Blizzard Pass

Blizzard Pass

T. V. Olsen

This Large Print edition is published by Thorndike Press®,
Waterville, Maine USA and by BBC Audiobooks, Ltd,
Bath, England.

Published in 2004 in the U.S. by arrangement with
Golden West Literary Agency.

Published in 2004 in the U.K. by arrangement with
Golden West Literary Agency.

U.S. Hardcover 0-7862-6704-6 (Western)
U.K. Hardcover 1-4056-3123-6 (Chivers Large Print)
U.K. Softcover 1-4056-3124-4 (Camden Large Print)

The text of this Large Print edition is unabridged.
Other aspects of the book may vary from the original edition.

Set in 16 pt. Plantin by Elena Picard.

Printed in the United States on permanent paper.

British Library Cataloguing-in-Publication Data available

Library of Congress Cataloging-in-Publication Data

Olsen, Theodore V.
    Blizzard Pass / T. V. Olsen.
        p. cm.
    ISBN 0-7862-6704-6 (lg. print : hc : alk. paper)
    1. Outlaws — Fiction. 2. Blizzards — Fiction. 3. Ghost
towns — Fiction. 4. Large type books. I. Title.
PS3565.L8B49 2004
813'.54—dc22   2004042277

1

The quick mountain twilight was rushing down as the Raven brothers came in sight of Cernak's station. They had ridden down the pass from the east, and the blizzard was out of the north. Snow whitened their right sides from hats to boots, mounding on the right side of their hat brims. Their whiskers were frosted stiff on that side, and their horses' right flanks were caked white. The storm was incredibly fierce for the season's first. It beat at the two hunched riders with bony fists, as if with a conscious intent to smash down the men and their mounts.

The sky was a flinty, churning gray like dirty surf. It had built from a few streaky banners of cloud at noon to a massed, scudding darkness that pounded out of the north ahead of heavy winds. Less than two hours ago the first mild eddying flakes had begun. Now the season's first snowfall was turning into a full-fledged blizzard.

The lashing cold bit through Milt Raven's old canvas mackinaw, cutting him to the bone. He and his horse leaned against the blasting snow, which filled their eyes and noses and mouths like icy dust.

His brother, Cullin, yelled from behind him, "Milt, is that it?"

"Has to be," Milt shouted back.

A scatter of ancient buildings hulked darkly through the pelting curtain of snow. Only one of them showed lights, and that would be the swing station.

Thirty Mile, they called it — this high, deserted old town that boasted the last station on the High Mountain Stage Company line, which ended thirty miles away at Silverton — thirty miles of hairpin road skirting under soaring cliffs and around plunging gorges.

Once — so they had learned back in Saintsburg — Thirty Mile had been a lush boomtown, spilling over its mountain-cupped brim with gold fever, hard cash, easy sin. It still squatted like a black, immovable scab midway along the broad, hill-shouldered floor of Blizzard Pass. For the town had been built quickly of the giant pines that conveniently mantled every slope. There was hardly a board of milled lumber in the place, so that Thirty

Mile had not blown away before the fierce winds that tore through the pass all year around. Deserted, it had simply collapsed in quiet ruin.

But there was a small profit to be realized by anybody caring to maintain a roadhouse at this point. Until winter clogged the high passes, there was always a steady trickle of emigrant trains, escort troops, miners, trappers, and ordinary travelers. Winter also put a period to the irregular runs of the High Mountain Stage Company, which had for years engaged the roadhouse proprietor to service their line.

Anton Cernak, so the talk went, had taken over the roadhouse and swing station last spring, at about the same time he'd sent money to Poland to bring his daughter and grandson to America.

The tracks of the stage wheels were still fresh and sharp in the snow as Milt and Cullin followed them to the lee side of the station. Two men were unhitching the Concord's team. The horses stood snuffling and blowing. Their coats were shaggy with winter fur, their rumps silvered with snow.

One man left off working and tramped over to meet the riders.

A mighty wedge of a fellow, with taper-

9

ing hips and bulky shoulders, he had a heavy Slavic face capped by a bushing thatch of brown hair that had long ago sunwashed to a bleached shade piebald with gray. He was bareheaded, muffled in a thick, striped blanket coat, his hands rammed deep in the pockets.

"Big as a bear and twice as surly," was how Shallot had described this man. It fit. You knew it even before he spoke in a gruff and grudging manner.

"I'm Cernak. Do some'at for you?"

"Name's Raven. Milt Raven. My brother, Cullin, here. Like something to eat and some care for our horses."

"Supper's almost on. Stage just got in. Want to put up for the night?"

"Don't reckon," Raven said. "Bit of grub will do us."

"Gabe!" Cernak turned his shaggy head toward the stock tender. "You see to their horses. I'll finish the unhitching." He looked back at Raven. "Go on in. Help yourself to a drink, eh?"

The stock tender took their reins. He was a clumsy, gentle-looking youth, with pale, shallow eyes and evidently less than half his wits.

They moved to the door. Milt worked up the latch with a numb finger. Cullin hissed

10

exultantly in his brother's ear, "That's him, all right! Ain't it?"

"That's him."

The wind gave a fierce yank at the door as Raven freed the latch. The door swung in to slam against the wall.

They ducked inside quickly. Raven started to wrestle the door shut, but a man grunted, "Get by the fire. I'll see t'this."

They crossed the room to the nearest fireplace with stiff, beaten steps. For a half minute they just stood, turning their bodies to the warmth. Their faces were chapped raw and held the dazed, unthawed looks of men whipped numb by hours of slashing weather.

Milt Raven tugged off his gloves with his teeth and beat his hands together. He unfastened the buttons of his mackinaw, then untied the scarf that anchored down his hat. His hair glinted almost white, cropped close and tight to the lean shape of his skull. His features were sharply planed and angled like granite. His mouth was thin and incisive, his eyes ice-blue.

As he shucked off his mackinaw he glanced around the common room.

It was broad and long, with a puncheon floor and two big fireplacs that did not — in this weather — make the place overly

11

warm. The furnishings were comfortable and plain. The one touch of grandeur was a tarnished chandelier, probably salvaged from one of the old dance halls. It was suspended by its brass chain from a crossbeam, fanning a wan halo of candlelight.

A man and a woman were sitting at a long trestle table brightened by a red-and-white-checked oilcloth. They were trying politely not to stare at Raven, but he was used to it. People always did at first.

Minus his bulky mackinaw, he was undiminished, filling his hickory shirt and rawhide vest with a rawboned power. Huge-boned, he was gaunt as a cougar. He looked gigantic and looming in the exaggerated dance of firelight.

The man who had closed the door came over, thrusting out his hand. "I'm O'Herlihy, the driver. You lads must o' been close behind the stage. Queer I didn't catch a sight o' you back on the flats before the storm turned fierce."

It was a half-question.

Milt guessed O'Herlihy to be about thirty, not tall but thickset and powerful in his vast buffalo coat. His broad face glowed like autumn apples with the cold, and was framed in a curly mat of blue-black beard that wore a fringe of dripping icicles.

12

He had a grip like iron. Milt met it without much trouble, but he noticed that Cullin couldn't keep from wincing.

"I guess we caught up pretty fast the last few miles," Milt said. "Milt Raven. My brother, Cullin."

"Ah" — O'Herlihy swept him with a twinkling and boisterous gaze — "you're a broth of a man, Mr. Raven."

You'd think he had just finished a sulky trot around a graded track on a fair day instead of a brutal, bitter haul over the High Mountain route's most rugged stretch, handling a heavy Concord and a team of rawboned brutes. He waved cheerily at the man and the woman.

"The Reverend Mr. James Parnell and his missus, these are. My passengers."

The Parnells stood and came forward, a gracious pair. They were nothing like the rawboned sin-shouters and their slatternly wives who made the circuits in this country.

The minister was blond, in his early thirties, but he looked very boyish and clean-cut. He had an easy, cultivated voice. He was gently polite and wore a clean shirt with his nankeen trousers and tweedy belted traveler's coat.

Aimee Parnell was an olive-skinned girl

with very black hair, very green eyes, and features of a cameo delicacy. Her dress of soft brown muslin was modest and inexpensive, yet she wore it with a queenly elegance. In this rugged country she seemed almost unreal — a small, exquisite doll of a woman. Her voice was low and lilting, accented French.

O'Herlihy waved the brothers over to the plank bar that occupied the north end of the room. On it stood a solitary keg and a row of tin cups. The driver hefted the keg, uncorked it, and spilled pale liquor into three of the cups. He glanced at the Parnells, who had returned to the table.

"You'll join us, Reverend?"

"No. Thanks." Parnell smiled. He looked half apologetic, half ill-at-ease.

He was a curious one, Raven thought. All the preachers he'd ever met would have called damnation on O'Herlihy for his brash invitation.

Wind thundered down the pass. Windows rattled in their casings; timbers creaked. A closed door on the room's south wall led to the kitchen. Raven could hear a rich crackle of frying meat, and an aroma of fresh coffee reached clear to the bar. He heard a woman's voice back there, and a small boy's. The daughter, that

14

would be — and the grandson.

It was pleasant to be standing here, arms crossed on the bar while he blotted up the room's warmth and cauterized his gut with the good fire of Cernak's potent white mule.

O'Herlihy refilled their cups. He said cheerfully, "You'll be staying over the night, Mr. Raven?"

Raven shook his head. "We came over the pass clear from Saintsburg. Got important business in Silverton. Best we get there by morning."

"You're daft," O'Herlihy said. "No offense. But it's a night for white owls — of which I seen one only this afternoon. Silverton's thirty mile away. You'll ride all night to make her. Hear that blizzard? A stemwinder for fair. She'll blow till she blows herself out. Maybe all night, maybe another day and more. I was going to say that we'll be laying over till tomorrow if not the next day."

"I was counting on being in Silverton tomorrow," James Parnell said. "Are you sure?"

"Man, I'm sure. Them sinholes'll be waiting for you same later as now, Reverend. Listen to that wind."

"The snow didn't seem very deep."

15

"She's added a couple o' inches since we got here. We'd go a fair ways and then find ourselves stalled to the axles in a drift. About halfway between here and Silverton, and a fifteen-mile hike either way. Snow climbing to our knees and temperatures dropping fast. Nagh! Be a fool risk to go on while this weather holds."

"Well, we're in your hands, Mr. O'Herlihy. In this country I suppose that a stage driver is a little like a ship's captain. His word being law to his people . . ."

O'Herlihy gave a rich bray of laughter. The idea suited him immensely.

Raven gazed thoughtfully into his cup. Neither Shallot nor any of them had counted on the blizzard — nor on the driver and passengers staying over. And this O'Herlihy was a tough potato, or he missed his guess.

Extra trouble or not, he knew that none of these things would make one damned particle of difference to Captain George Shallot . . .

The kitchen door opened. The woman came briskly out, carrying a pile of tin plates. She gave the men at the bar a fleeting glance.

That was enough to bring her to a dead halt. Startled, she relaxed her hold on the plates. Most of them slipped from her hands and went clanging to the floor.

Milt realized with a sudden discomfort that she was staring straight at him. Her eyes were so wide you could see the whites around the brown irises. Her face was pale with a stunned, deathly shock.

O'Herlihy went over to her, cup in hand. "What's ailing you, Anna mavournin?"

"Nothing. Is nothing!"

She tore her tense stare from Milt Raven's face and dropped to her knees on the floor. She began gathering up the plates. Clucking his tongue, O'Herlihy stooped to help her.

"Man," Cullin murmured, "that there does make a man's sweet tooth ache."

Milt gave him a hard glance. But Cullin was watching the woman.

Cullin was nowhere near his brother's size, but he had a big catty build. He seemed a modified version of Milt Raven in every respect. The older brother's harsh, fierce look was toned down in Cullin to a lean, jaunty ruggedness. He had the same pale hair and light blue eyes.

He humidly absorbed the woman's movements as she irritably circled the table, clattering the dishes into place. O'Herlihy assisted with a flourish, then used the oc-

17

casion to give her a quick squeeze around the waist. He leaped back with a bray of laughter, but not before her hand caught his jaw in a ringing slap.

"My, you're a lovely Polack," O'Herlihy laughed.

A small and bright-eyed boy ran out of the kitchen to see what was happening. He started laughing, too.

"Ladislas!" His mother's face was flushed and angry. "Get two more plates."

"*Da,* Little Mother!" The boy popped back into the kitchen.

O'Herlihy kissed his hand to her and swaggered back to the bar, chuckling. He gave the two brothers a broad wink.

"Ain't she a big lovely Polack, though? Mrs. Anna Kosciusko, it is. *Missus* with great force, though her good man's dead these several years. A score of times I asked her to be Mrs. O'Herlihy, and it's nagh. Always nagh. Why look, mavournin, here's a preacher and —"

"Pah! Fool Irish!"

She stood with hands on hips, eyes darkly blazing, and she was a marvelous picture, all right. As tall as most men, but with a strong womanly shape. It had that lean, exciting maturity that preserved a woman's figure long beyond her twenty-

18

seven or twenty-eight years.

O'Herlihy roared with giant mirth as she stalked back to the kitchen. Both the Parnells smiled, but they were embarrassed.

The candles guttered crazily as the outside door swung open. Cernak and Gabe floundered in with an icy rush of wind and snow. Cernak held the door shut while the stock tender latched it and swung a dangling crossbar into place for added security.

Milt Raven took note of that crossbar — and of the heavy wooden shutters that covered every window. All these details made extra hitches in the plan, but that was why he and Cullin were here. To single out strengths and weaknesses in the place — the people.

Anna carried in the steaming dishes of steaks and beans and biscuits. The men took their places around the table. The chairs were massive hand-carved affairs with basketwoven seats and backs made of stretched rawhide thongs.

Everyone looked at Parnell, and he gave a vague start, then said a short grace.

The minister and his wife made gracious small talk during the meal, though they obviously weren't in a mood for it. They talked to the stockboy, who spoke haltingly of his beloved horses and beamed with pleasure. They gently joshed the little boy, Laddie. They drew his mother into their talk, seeming not to mind her stumbling English and abashed manner.

She was continually getting up and hurrying to the kitchen on trivial errands that kept her away from the table most of the time. Raven realized that she was bitterly aware, beside Aimee Parnell's china-doll loveliness, of her own bigness and reddened hands and shabby clothes.

For a fact, Anna Kosciusko was not even pretty. Her face was prominently boned, a shade too long and narrow, the nose proudly but not becomingly arched, lips full but compressed and severe, dark brown hair drawn to the back of her neck in a hard, smooth bun. Her skirt of heavy cotton twill was faded and threadbare, her worn, unflattering shirt probably an old one of her father's.

What she also had was that fine, lean body, strong-hipped and broad-shouldered, the long, quick legs, wide-set breasts that were full and thrusting, and a skin as darkly clear as strained honey. Too bad she seemed unable or unwilling to take account of one fact — that she was a young

Amazon whose earthy vitality simply washed Aimee Parnell out of the room.

After that first startled reaction to him, Raven noticed that she avoided even a glance in his direction. He was sure this wasn't accidental. He was still puzzled by the whole business — and a little worried.

"Reverend" — O'Herlihy stowed a mouthful of steak in his cheek and chewed like a contemplative bull — "you say you're going no farther'n Silverton. I find that a curiosity."

Parnell smiled. "Protestant shortage?"

"Not a bit, sir. Place is lousy with 'em — um, no offense. Just they ain't the sweet churchly souls you knew back home, wherever —"

"Boston."

"Unh. Every Irishman knows where *that* is. But Silverton, now. Ones there who'll hear out a preacher want him to have 'em turning on the hot spit o' Sheol. Folks sin strong, they want preaching that's stiffer'n vinegar."

"So I've been told," Parnell said quietly. "That's why . . . well, no matter. Silverton will be our new home."

He gave his wife a brief glance; she lowered her eyes. Raven hadn't noticed it before, but he did now. There was something

21

wrong between these two.

Cernak looked at Raven. "Be better you fellows stay over. Storm is too fierce to ride out the pass tonight."

Raven looked up, his eyes as impersonal as a snake's. He guessed that Cernak's only interest in them was as a pair of paying guests — and it made a chance to get the information they really needed without touching the Pole's suspicions.

"I count four of you here," Raven said. "Add a driver, two passengers. With us, nine. You got that many beds?"

"Sure, sure." Cernak waved a hairy hand. "No worry. Look, I sleep in the loft, Gabe shares my room. Anna and the boy got a bed in the room off the kitchen. That door" — he nodded toward a door on the west wall — "goes to a dog trot, leads out to the annex, which is where you put up. Got a drape in the middle. Nice and private for the preacher and his wife on one side, you boys and driver on the other. Clean beds, reasonable rates — eh?"

Raven lifted a forkful of beans and held it poised, as if he were thinking this over. Finally he shook his head. "I don't reckon. I been over that road. We'll tough it through all right."

"It is foolish," Cernak growled. "Even if

there's not the blizzard, it's plenty dark. Down on the flats, where it's blowed over, you could easy lose the road."

"We'll tough it through."

"You want very much to get on, mister," Anna snapped.

Raven looked at her in surprise. She had not even spoken to him during the meal, much less met his eyes. Now she was doing both, a chill hostility in her face.

"Yeah, ma'am. We got kind of important business in Silverton. Too crowded here. Don't want to put you people out none."

"I no think this bother a man like you so much. And what is your business is so important, eh?"

Her father cleared his throat at her in a half-warning bellow. Anna Kosciusko was unperturbed. She said calmly, "I get the pie," and rose and walked to the kitchen with Cullin's hot, moist stare following her.

She was a fine cook. The deep-dish apple pie was delicious. But it was like sawdust in Raven's mouth. Where she had refused to look at him before, she now sat across from him and never took her eyes off his face.

Could she suspect something? No, that was impossible. He and Cullin had never seen any of these people before tonight, including Anna Kosciusko.

Yet she kept watching him that same way till the meal was finished. And there was no mistaking the expression in her eyes.

It was hatred. Pure icy hatred.

2

"Yessir," Cullin sang out, "that big Polack gal surely does make a man's sweet tooth ache." Raven glanced back. His brother was a dim, jogging shape a couple of yards behind him. Raven didn't reply. "All right, all right," Cullin said surlily.

"We had enough of that," Raven said. "Don't start it up again. You hear?"

No answer. He heard, all right.

Raven said, "Let's get on," and kneed his grullo into a bucking lunge against the drifting snow.

Voices carried easily between the high, steep walls here, where the storm's violence was broken. But after that brief exchange there was no more talk.

A relief to escape the slashing wind for a while, but the snow was banking more swiftly between these cramped walls than in the open, sifting down in thick gusts off the rimrock. It was getting harder for the horses to break trail.

Then they were out of the stretch of tight-walled gorge, and the howling din of blizzard engulfed them again. Faintly to either side lifted long, easy flanks of hills darkened by a piney overgrowth that was starting to blur into the general whiteness. All was white but the black-sided hulks of boulders erupted by the fall freezes and thaws from ancient resting places and sent crashing into the road. Those obstructing stage passage had been rolled out of the way.

Despite the darkness, the whipping flail of snow, they had no trouble feeling their way. The snow-hidden road followed a natural demarcation looping around the bases of the giant slopes.

Also the prints of their passing an hour earlier still faintly showed. For the brothers were not moving west along Blizzard Pass toward the lowlands and Silverton. They were heading back the way they had come.

Raven leaned against the wind, chin down, and let the horse have his head, bucking the drifts. His short-coupled grullo took it in contemptuous stride, better than Cullin's Virginia hunter, which was wholly unfit for breasting a high-country winter. Cullin had no damned sense when it came to buying a horse.

Cullin had no damned sense, period.

Raven pulled deeply into his mackinaw, feeling bone-deep weary from more than a long, cold, punishing day in the saddle.

A hell of a thing for a man to reach thirty-three and find himself still wet-nursing a kid brother. Not such a kid either. Cullin was twenty-six. But to Milt Raven he was still *the kid,* as he had been since they had been orphaned boys living with a crusty and indifferent uncle in St. Joe. Cullin's nose-thumbing antics had forced Milt into a thousand battles. Always Cullin would taunt and torment some playmate until the boy would turn on him. Then Cullin would yowl, and Milt would come to give the bully what for.

That had gone on a long while before Milt came to recognize a fine strategy behind Cullin's provocations. He always made damned sure that his big brother was in earshot, and he never provoked anybody quite his size or smaller. It was always some kid a few hairs larger, giving him the excuse to holler for Milt.

There was that when they were kids, and later there were the women, and not much to be done in either case. Once, fed up to the ears, Milt had ridden away to let Cullin

27

worry himself out of his scrapes. But when word reached him that Cullin was in trouble, he had promptly returned to bail him out.

At the time he had come to a bitter awareness that for him, anyway, blood was thicker than vinegar. Somebody had to take care of Cullin, somebody would always have to, and there was nobody else. Then, sour as the admission had tasted, watching over a younger brother had become an ingrained way of life. The years passed; the tired road grew longer. You no longer pictured another way of life. Your young dreams turned drab and frayed, and finally you grew a callus of indifference.

Sometimes, as now, Raven looked back and dredged up a lukewarm regret. If he had it to do over and could have seen where it would lead, he might have done differently. Might have. But even if the kid had been made to fight his own fights and take his lumps, there would have been the women later. And other things.

What the hell, anyhow. Tired like this, a man was prey to wishful thoughts. You couldn't change two facts. One — Cullin was Cullin. Two — it was too late for turning back.

Abruptly through the blowing snow

Raven saw the black, sharp spire of basalt. He had been watching for it on the road flank, for it marked where he and Cullin had come onto the road a couple of hours ago. The prints were all but blown over by now, and except for that lone black upthrust the whole landscape was a dreary anonymity of white veined by dark, exposed angles of rocks.

Raven swung off the road and sent the grullo plunging up the slope, Cullin behind him. The steady wind had kept the snow broomed shallow on this regular hillside, but it was still a steep climb. Twice Raven felt the grullo's hooves slip on bare patches of shale.

They reached the hill's summit. It was thickly covered by a mixture of spruce and short-topped jackpine. Raven put his animal into the heart of this low-growing tangle. Suddenly they were shielded from the wind again. Strongly shadowed on the snow under the packed trees was a trail of horse tracks winding back along a fairly clear corridor. At the same time that a whiff of pine smoke hit his nostrils, Raven saw the diffused light of a fire; it knifed orange streamers between the trees. Another hundred feet and men's faint voices mingled with the moan of wind.

"Quién es?" a man called sharply.

"Us, Billy."

"Ho, Milton! Ride in, good amigos."

A man's slim and wiry form moved cat-like out of the dark obscurity of trees to the right of them. As you'd expect, Billy Mendez had been the first to note their approach and prepare accordingly.

Billy grinned cheerfully. "This she-blizzard is a real bucket of hell, ain't she, amigos?"

Cullin laughed. "You figure this storm's a woman, hey?"

"Sure. Feel them long, mean claws she's digging in? A real bitch. Jésus Kareesto, you boys look froze. Come up by fire."

Billy walked ahead of them, Winchester swinging in his fist. They entered a wide clearing.

The sheltered camp was set under an overhang of granite shelving out from the tall cliff to one side. Otherwise the tight young trees hemmed it all around. Dirty snow that floored the clearing was tramped into the loam by booted feet. Saddles and saddlebags and bedrolls were scattered in the lee of the overhang; a picket rope stretched between trees held four horses.

"You hombres are beat out good," Billy Mendez told the brothers. "Get up by fire. I take your horses."

They handed him their reins and walked to the fire and settled on their heels. Their hands were numb as blocks. They yanked off fleece-lined gloves with their teeth and turned their hands to the blaze.

A slight man of forty was crouched across the fire from them. "Well?"

Raven ignored him for the moment. Red-hot prickles were shooting through his clumsily stiff hands. He worked the fingers slowly. Then he pulled a glove back on and picked up the battered coffeepot from the edge of the fire. Finding a charred cup, he threw out the dregs and filled it. He drank off half the scalding, murky brew and handed the rest to Cullin.

Only then did he look at Captain George Shallot, noticing the hot deep-set anger in his eyes with no concern. Shallot didn't like being ignored, but he took it from Raven and said nothing.

Shallot's narrow, bony face seemed too small for his pale, domelike brow. He was hatless and even under crudest conditions he kept his thin, graying hair neatly combed to hide a receding hairline. His face might have been that of an ascetic or intellectual. The eyes were something else. They burned like recessed coals. The little

31

pouches of flesh hooding them at the outer corners lent him a kind of brooding malignity. There was a quivering energy about him that reminded you of a lean hound in leash.

He said, "What about this Cernak fellow?"

"He's the one," Raven said. "Fits your description of your man Rolvinski to a T."

Shallot grunted a soft "Ah" in the tone of a man shutting his fist over something elusive. He turned his head. "Quintus! Do you want to hear this?"

Quintus Terrill, Shallot's lieutenant, had been dozing on his bedroll back in a deep niche of the cliff. Now he sat up, yawned, ran his hands through his thick, light hair, rolled out of his blankets, stood up, and came to the fire.

He was a large, tall man with an easy, leonine way of moving, despite a missing right arm. His empty mackinaw sleeve was tucked into his belt. About Shallot's age, his face had gone somewhat fleshy under its pale beard stubble, but his gray and luminous eyes were still rather eagerly pleasant. Behind them, the soul of a born romantic looked on the world through lenses pearled by dead memories.

Terrill sat down on a folded blanket,

crossed his legs tailor-fashion, and gave the Ravens a mild nod. The others pulled close around the fire, too. Billy Mendez, having tended to the horses, stood hipshot with his rifle still dangling from one hand, the other hand thumb-hooked in his belt, eyes half-shuttered against smoke from the brown cigarillo tilted in his lopsided grin.

Dolph Smith also edged up by the fire and squatted down, keeping a slight but noticeable distance from the others. He was an ex-slave, a black, rawboned hawk of a man with a face like a mahogany mask and a big crooked blade of a nose. Squatting, his long legs doubled up, he looked like a big smoky grasshopper with its leaping limbs attached in reverse. He had a couple of heavy wool blankets wrapped around him over his sheepskin, but his teeth still chattered. Dolph was always cold.

Rounding out the party was a fattish fellow of thirty-five with a loutish, cheerful look, a baby's blue, innocent eyes, a face chapped and puffy from weather, and hair like a stack of drake-tailed straw. He was known to the others only as "Albie" and he had a dog's loyalty to Shallot. All of them but the Raven brothers had been with Shallot a long time.

"Me too, huh, Cap'n George?"

"Of course you too, Albie," Shallot said with his dry, febrile chuckle. "Milt is going to tell us what we need to know, so keep your ears open —"

A retching spasm of coughing doubled him up. When it subsided, he was pale and gasping; he motioned for Raven to continue.

Raven smoothed a sooty patch of snow and with a stick diagramed the layout of Cernak's roadhouse. He sketched in different rooms, explained the sleeping arrangements. Wind snaked under the overhang, guttering the fire.

Quintus Terrill was uneasy. "I don't like it, George," he said in his soft Tidewater drawl. "This blizzard complicates things as is. We may have a time getting out afterward. And now these passengers and driver staying over. Makes three more people to handle."

"What do you suggest?" Shallot asked.

"That we wait a day. Those three will be going on tomorrow. By then the blizzard should have passed."

"Suppose it hasn't?" Shallot snapped. "Even if it has, the snow will be too deep by morning for the stage to roll."

"Then they'll leave horseback, no doubt.

34

The point is, George, that three extra people mean that much more risk. To us — to them."

"I always avoid trouble when trouble can be avoided. But I look at the stakes first, the chances second. Don't be such an old woman, Quintus. I've taken every precaution, even to sending Milt and Cullin to scout the premises. Now we can take 'em in a walk."

"The blizzard, amigos." Billy Mendez huddled deeper in his frayed sheepskin as another icy blast whipped the fire. "She is a bucket of hell."

"Exactly," Shallot murmured. "The storm might last for days. They might be marooned — us too. Difference is they'll be snug as bedbugs while we're freezing off our tails out here. Temperature's dropped fast all day and still plunging." He shook his head. "It's unseasonable. Weather's all wrong. I don't like the feel of it. Best we find shelter at once. That means the station."

Terrill said worriedly, "Suppose the weather holds bad, and we can't get out afterward?"

"We stay till we can get out."

"But we'll have to share the place with seven people, all waiting a chance to get us! And for how long?"

"Well, how in hell should I know, Quintus?" Shallot said wearily. "We couldn't foresee a blizzard like this so early in the season. Caught us unawares. Unfortunate, but we have to take it in stride. And perhaps any number of other hitches before we're done."

"Man," Dolph Smith growled, "what we up against anyways? Couple women, little boy, a preacher, stage driver, and a dumbhead stockboy. Ain't none of 'em grand odds. Onliest one we got to really watch is Rolvinski or Cernak, whatever's his goddam name. If they's one dangerous 'un, he's it."

"Dolph's right," Shallot said. "The Polack's not really clever, but shrewd as a weasel. And strong as a bull. Remember how he once broke a two-inch pine board between his hands?"

"*Si*," said Mendez. "He is a bucket of hell, that big bear. But I'm think that we pull his teeth, these other, they be no trouble."

"Don't underrate the stage driver," Raven said. "That Irishman looked like he could take on his weight in wildcats, was he riled once."

"All right," Shallot said impatiently.

36

"We'll have a couple of tough ones to worry about. I think we might just manage. The storm, the night, and surprise — those are our allies, gentlemen." His grin gave him a death's-head look. "But procrastination and discussion are not. Shall we away?"

There was a feverish haste to the way they threw their gear together and saddled their mounts. For five of them, tonight marked the end of a long, bitter search.

Dolph swung to saddle and settled his skinny shanks in place, muttering, "I never did trust that goddam Polack."

Shallot said, "Oh, come along, Dolph." He gave the others a solemn wink. "Fact is, Dolph's missed the old Polack since he skinned out on us. Long as he was around, Dolph felt he was coming up in the world."

Mendez cackled. Dolph turned his masked stare briefly on Shallot, then put his eyes front and clucked his horse into motion. Dolph hated all white men, but he hated Shallot and Terrill, both castoffs of the Old South's decayed gentry, more than any.

For that matter, Raven thought, there was no love lost between any of them, except Shallot and Terrill, who had been chums since boyhood; and of course Collin and himself.

It was not friendship, not even companionship, that linked the six men. It was more like a joint quarantine. For with nothing else in common, all had a rancid awareness of one fact: the gang was the only home they'd ever know.

By the time they reached Thirty Mile, all were numbed by the storm's blast. Leaning into the wind like canting statues, hardly able to feel the rocking plod of their mounts, they rode down the crooked lane of street past old, sagging buildings, which stood against this storm as they had a hundred others.

The ramshackle livery barn that now housed Cernak's swing teams loomed to their right, perhaps a couple hundred feet from the roadhouse. When the brothers had ridden away, they were far up the pass before the windows of Cernak's station had ceased to make wan beacons through the storm. Now the lights were extinguished, the heavy shutters secured. All were abed.

The wind seemed to gather strength, booming and echoing from the depths of Blizzard Pass. It shrieked like a dying horse. The men dismounted now and fought their way across a last few dozen feet to the barn, almost carried off their feet by the gale-force blasts.

Raven shouted to Cullin. The two passed their reins to the others, then lifted the heavy bar anchoring the barn's double doors. It took all their weight and strength to wrestle open the doors, hold them while the others led the animals inside, and then haul them shut. Raven held them that way while Cullin angle-wedged the bar between floor and doors.

Total darkness in the barn. You could hear horses' restive stamping, crackle of straw; there was a musty reek of hay and dung and ammonia.

"Hold on," Raven said.

He located by feel the lantern hanging from a stall upright. Before taking it down, he beat his gloved hands together, simultaneously stamping his feet, to restore sensation. Then, hands still as unfeeling as ice chunks, he fumbled out the folded oilcloth containing his matches. He struck two misfires; the third match took flame but whiffed out in the wind that cut like whining blades through the numerous chinks.

"Man, get that frigging thing lighted," Dolph growled. "I get the willies, all this dark."

"Keep your hide on," Raven said. "It's all one shade."

Billy Mendez tittered.

On the fourth try Raven got the lantern lighted. The sickly rays ate away part of the dark, picking out a clay runway and crude stalls.

Shallot looked half frozen, hanging on to his pommel to keep his legs from folding. Now he was slipping down, no strength left in his numb fingers. At the same time he was doubled by a coughing fit. Billy Mendez stepped over to help him.

"Keep your goddam greaser hands off me," Shallot snarled. "Quintus!"

Billy grinned and stepped back, mildly shrugging his lifted palms. He took offense at almost nothing.

Terrill lent the leader a supporting arm, leading him to the side of the runway and settling him on a pile of straw, his back against a stall partition. Shallot sat with his eyes closed, his face white under its ruddy splotching of frostbite.

Raven held the lantern high while the others beat arms against their sides like demented roosters and stamped circulation back to their legs.

"Wha zis?" a strange voice whimpered.

The sound froze every man in place. They exchanged blank looks.

Raven thought the voice had come from

the rear of the stables. Faintly now, he heard straw crackle and slither. He took a couple of steps down the runway. Lantern-light reached into the far shadows.

"Who's there?" he called.

A dark form rose out of an end stall and lurched into the runway.

Raven recognized Gabe, Cernak's handyman. The half-loonie. Raven's thoughts hit a startled blank. What in hell's he doing out here?

Gabe shuffled forward, a thick and muffled figure in the heavy blankets he held wrapped around him. Wisps of straw dripped from him as if he'd been sleeping half-buried in a mound of hay. His black, bristly hair was awry. He blinked fishily at them.

His brain started to function muddily. "What you doing here?" he shrilled.

Suddenly he shed the blankets. He'd been clutching something beneath them. Light skimmed along the upswinging barrels of a long shotgun.

Raven shouted, "Watch out!"

He was nearest the loonie and had to move fast; the Greener would chop him in half at this range. He flung himself sideways just in time. Shadows leaped and gyrated. He dropped inside the half-shelter of a stall, the hay cushioning his fall.

The others were caught off guard, still awkward and lead-footed with cold, facing the lethal menace of a scramble-brained kid bringing up a shotgun while they couldn't even begin to get their coats clawed open and their guns out.

The Greener's low bellow caromed through the barn. A man screamed — a high, fluting sound of pain and terror. That was Billy Mendez.

3

The horses were whickering and stamping with fear. Raven had a momentary impression of the other men scattering to right and left out of the runway. At the same instant he tore his Stetson free of the scarf holding it and dropped it over the lantern, wiping out the light. The shotgun roared again, with a lurid splash of flame. Raven heard the raking splatter of shot rattle against the partition of his stall hardly a foot above his head but on the other side.

On the heel of that shot a six-shooter crashed twice, both flashes close to the floor.

A soggy grunt. Something heavy made a slow sodden crash in the straw.

Outside, the wind screamed unbrokenly. Inside, except for Mendez' sporadic moans of agony, there was a musty stillness now.

"I think I got him," came Dolph's hollow voice.

Raven eased onto his haunches and

lifted his Stetson off the lantern. The scene flickered back. Dolph was down on one knee, his mackinaw hanging open. He had torn it in one powerful yank to get out his Colt. The gun gleamed in his black fist, still leveled.

The boy Gabe was crumpled in the straw on his back, the shotgun laying across his belly at an angle. Raven could not tell any more from here, and now he came to his feet for a better look.

"Wait," Shallot said hoarsely, "douse that light again!"

Instantly Raven dropped the Stetson over the lantern and set it on the clay floor, shutting off all light but a pinkish glow of the hat's crown.

Shallot was right: the storm's fury might or might not have drowned out the shots. Even if the sounds had faintly reached the roadhouse, probably only the lightest of sleepers would be roused. But if even one person had been roused, the men in the barn would know in a few minutes.

"All of you stay still," Shallot murmured. "Billy, goddammit, stop whining!"

"I can't help it," Mendez sobbed. "My leg, she's busted to hell. Oh, Jesus, but she hurt, amigos!"

"Shut up!"

For a good ten minutes they crouched in the cold and darkness, listening. Below the shrieking onrun of wind were the small, restless noises of uneasy horses, occasional cough or mutter from one of the men and other sounds from Mendez.

Finally Shallot said, "All right, Milt. Let's have a look."

Raven replaced the Stetson on his head and joined Shallot beside the motionless body of the stock tender. Except for the gaping wound in his throat, he looked as if he had gone quietly to sleep on the floor. Shallot prodded him with a toe; his flesh was loose and inert.

"Who in hell was he?"

"Kid who took care of the horses."

"Thought you said he's the one slept in the loft with the Polack."

"So I was told. Don't ask me what he was doing out here." Raven shrugged. "Kid seemed odd in the head, that's all I know."

Terrill had come up. "Christ, George," he said.

"Don't say it," Shallot murmured. "It's happened, Quintus, and it's done."

"But God, George! Clockwork, you said. We're not in the house yet, and a man's already dead!"

Shallot said, "So he is," and turned on his heels to fix a stare on them all. "It doesn't change a goddam thing. We're going on according to plan."

Dolph's face was expressionless; Cullin looked faintly excited; Albie looked fatly blank — that was all. Outside of Terrill, nobody seemed perturbed by what had happened.

Raven knew that he alone shared Terrill's regret, but he was no romantic. He accepted this hapless killing and filed it away with the thousand other mistakes that could not be taken back. Shallot was right in this: it was done.

"For the love of the sweet God," Mendez whimpered, "will somebody look at my leg?"

Dolph knelt, took out his clasp knife and opened the large blade, and roughly ripped Mendez' rawhide *chiverras* up the side.

The right knee was a slick and darkly glistening butchery, mangled flesh and splintered bone pulped together. It had taken the full blast of the kid's first shot.

"Good Christ," Cullin whispered.

Mendez raised himself on his elbows to look. *"Por Dios!"* His face was livid.

"Don't look good for you, man," Dolph said indifferently. He folded up the blade and stood.

"What d'you mean? Dolph!"

"Never mind," Shallot cut in. "We can't see properly to your leg out here. Can't really tell anything till we get you in the house. A warm fire, Billy, a soft bed — a good stiff drink, eh?"

A kindly word from Shallot was so rare, it struck the Mexican's terror deeper. He was mute now, his face like gray wax.

For now, all they could do was lay Mendez on the straw, crudely tie off his wound, and heap the dead Gabe's blankets over him.

Tersely, Shallot outlined how they would do it. He and Albie would take Cernak in the loft, Quintus would tend to the preacher and his missus, Dolph and Cullin would handle the driver, Milt would see to Cernak's daughter and the little boy.

Shallot's way of splitting the duty might seem trifling, but on such trifles hung a quality of leadership. He wanted to see to their most important bag, Cernak, himself, and the slow Albie made a competent hand only when Shallot oversaw him. Quintus Terrill and Milt Raven were the ones to be trusted around women, hence their assignments. The sullen but dependable Dolph and the unpredictable Cullin made a tough, balanced matching.

Plunging back out into the blizzard, they secured the doors and made the short bitter dash to the leeside of the roadhouse.

Out of the wind, Raven sidled to the front window. He had suggested, and Shallot had agreed, that it was best to enter by this end of the building, which was fairly isolated from any sleeping area. He felt beneath his mackinaw for his heavy Bowie and thrust the thick-heeled blade between frame and casing, and pried upward. Wood splintered loudly. Raven didn't pause, knowing the storm would easily cover the sound. More pressure: the window lifted an inch. He inserted a gloved hand in the crack and powerfully lifted; the window gaped widely.

There were still two heavy shutters, shut and barred from the inside, to be passed. He pushed the knife between them and shoved sideways. There was no give; he felt the steel straining.

"Dolph, you got a Bowie. Get it in here."

Dolph produced his blade and worked it into the crack below Raven's, and they pried simultaneously. The securing bar snapped. The shutters opened to a touch.

"Quick," Shallot hissed.

Raven went through first, swinging his legs over the sill and dropping into the room. The others followed. Shallot was the last through. He closed the shutters and jammed them with a shard of the cracked bar.

The big common room was feebly lighted by crumbling cherry coals in the two fireplaces. Shallot took some short, thick tallow candle stubs from his coat pocket and handed them around; these would light the men to their areas of duty.

They separated, Terrill and Dolph and Cullin slipping into the dog trot to reach the annex where the driver and passengers were. Shallot and Albie began a delicate ascent of the loft ladder to surprise Cernak.

Raven stepped carefully into the kitchen, at once spotting the side door that opened into the daughter's room. A curtain of jutesacks sewn together covered the opening. Raven moved to it, his shadow flung huge and formless by the lighted stub of candle he held. Groaning timbers and an occasional frost-snapping board smothered his noises. He stirred the drapes aside and stepped into the room.

The shallow light picked them out: boy nestled close to his mother, her dark hair fanning loosely across the pillow. She looked absurdly young, as vulnerable as her son.

Seeing the candle stuck in a brass holder

on the commode, Raven touched his candle to its wick, then pinched out his own and dropped the wax stub in his pocket. Afterward he put his back to the wall and folded his arms, watching the sleeping pair. The ruckus would start in a moment. All he had to do was wait and watch them — candy from a baby.

A sudden sharpness of voices from the attic, underscored by Cernak's startled rumble. Then a gunshot, its heavy racket leaping from room to room.

Anna Kosciusko sat up, gasping. She put a hand to her throat. Candlelight pooled in her eyes; they dilated.

"You! What you do here?"

"Just stay quiet," Raven said.

Her son came awake with a sleepy, querulous mumble. Then his eyes opened wide. He stared fearlessly at Raven. Anna said something, not in English.

"You want to talk," Raven growled, "talk like white folks."

Shallot's voice, then Cernak's again, sounded in the loft. He saw Anna tilt her head, listening. But the drumming storm blurred the words. She eyed Raven warily and began to raise the bedclothes on the side away from him.

"Sit still."

She didn't reply, swinging her feet to the floor and never taking her eyes off him. She edged slowly along the wall toward the commode.

"I told you —"

She moved swiftly then, yanking open a drawer. Raven took one long step as she snatched inside the drawer and wheeled about. He caught her arm and twisted. The little .32 she held clattered to the floor.

She did not make a sound, but he felt her sag in his grasp. Her face was bloodless with the shock of pain. He realized that his unthinking violence had almost wrenched her arm from the socket. Letting her go now, he bent and scooped up the nickel-plated little gun and shoved it in his pocket.

At the same instant she tried to duck past him and reach the door. With a weary sort of growl, Raven clamped his arm around her waist and swung her clear of the floor. She kicked and struggled, and she was no lightweight, but he didn't want to hurt her again, and he couldn't let her lay hands on a weapon. Holding her literally tucked under his arm, he started for the door.

A flash of pain in his leg. Raven looked

down. The little boy had wrapped himself around his right leg like a small, active leech — one with teeth.

Raven strode grimly on through the kitchen, stiffly swinging his burdened leg. Anna continued to silently fight him, and she succeeded in twisting her body enough to reach his face with her hands. She beat at it as if driving nails with her fists. He blocked some of the blows with his free arm.

Reaching the common room, he dropped her on a bench, then set about prying the boy off his leg. As he dropped loose Anna stooped and snatched him up in her arms and stepped back.

"Is all right, is all right," she soothed him, eyes alive with hatred as she watched Raven. "I think you no should of bite him, though. We not know yet what poison is in him."

Raven looked uneasily away. Women embarrassed him. He had never been forward with them, but with a face like his it made no difference; they were just afraid of him. This one was, and she was anything but a woman who scared easily. In her case, though, he guessed it was connected with that curdling hatred of him that he couldn't understand.

Albie was descending the ladder now, and at the bottom he stood back, his gun ready, as Cernak came down. Shallot came last. He gave Raven, the woman, and the boy a brief glance, then said curtly, "Watch him, Albie," and strode to the turkey trot and called down the corridor, "Quintus!"

"All right," Terrill shouted.

"Who fired that shot?"

"The driver. He's fast — and tricky! Grabbed for Cullin's gun and it went off. Then Dolph buffaloed him."

"Get 'em out here."

Terrill appeared, gently prodding a half-dressed Reverend James Parnell ahead of him. The minister looked stunned; in his gentle world such things did not happen.

Dolph and Cullin came next, herding the stumbling driver. O'Herlihy was holding his head with both hands; blood streamed down the side of his face.

"Didn't Milt say the preacher had a wife? Where is she, Quintus?"

"She has to get dressed, George."

"You damned goose-livered fool!" Shallot spat. "She's alone in there? Perhaps digging a gun out of their luggage?"

"Come along, George! A preacher's wife . . . I think we can take that gamble."

"We can't afford any gamble! Not until

we've made a search for weapons. Now, you get the hell back in there and bring her out!"

O'Herlihy made a staggering half turn. "You bloody brute, you'll not —"

Dolph whipped his gun up and down, giving an explosive grunt of effort as he smashed it against O'Herlihy's skull. The driver plunged on his face across the splintered puncheons and didn't move.

Aimee Parnell stepped from the turkey trot at that moment. She was fully dressed, her face very white. "You cowards!" she said passionately. "Vile *cochons!*"

Weeping with anger, she dropped on her knees beside the unconscious driver. She tried to raise his head; she dabbed ineffectually at his bloody face with the hem of her skirt.

"James!" She looked up, eyes bright with tears. "James, you must do something!"

Her husband gave her a starkly pale stare. "And what, pray, do you suggest? Get myself killed, for instance?"

"Onward, Christian soldiers," Shallot said with a bony chuckle. He motioned with his gun. "I sincerely hope it won't become necessary to damage any more of you. But that is wholly your option. Now. Over by the wall, all of you."

He planted his hand in the center of Cernak's back. Muttering and glowering, the thickset Pole walked over to the bench and against the east wall.

Anna Kosciusko did not move. Standing proud and tall in her shapeless flannel gown, she held her son tightly to her. Her eyes blazed darkly.

"What you do here? What you want?"

"Presently," Shallot smiled. "Get over with that blue-ribbon daddy of yours, my girl. Now!"

She walked slowly to the bench and sat down, fiercely cradling Laddie to her, though the boy seemed as unafraid as his mother.

O'Herlihy groaned and moved; Aimee cried, "Oh, m'sieur, I fear your head is cracked."

"No more'n usual, dear lady." The driver waggled the head in question. "The Irish has a noodle like Cuchulain's fabled bull. Will you lend me a hand, Reverend?"

Between them, the Parnells helped the driver over to the bench. He eased down on it, groaning.

"You'll all stay as you are," Shallot said then, "till we've made a search of the house. Albie, remain here and keep your gun on them. If anyone stands up, shoot him."

"Yessir, Cap'n George." Albie yawned a vast grimace of pleasure.

"Dolph, Cullin, you'll fetch Billy from the barn. While you're about it, put up our horses. Then go back and bring all our gear in here — and don't forget that dead boy's shotgun."

"Dead," Anna echoed. A wild comprehension touched her face. "Gabe — is Gabe? He was out there — you kill him!"

Shallot gave a jaundiced nod. "Quintus, you and Milt and I will search this place top to bottom. Look for guns, knives, anything that might be used as a weapon. Then" — he looked at Anton Cernak, his smile tightening like a skull's grin — "we shall get to the business at hand."

4

A search of the rooms turned up, besides Anna's pistol and a Winchester rifle and a Colt .45 that Cernak kept under his loft bed but hadn't gotten a chance to use, an old Remington .44-40 in O'Herlihy's gear, and in the kitchen a cleaver and several wicked-looking butcher knives. Shallot ordered all of these brought to the common room and stacked in a corner, along with the gang's own rifles. Cullin and Dolph brought in Mendez, and Shallot told them to bunk him down in the annex. All of the gang's gear was transferred to the house.

Cullin entered by the kitchen while Milt was searching it. Dumping his and Milt's saddles on the floor, Cullin eyed his brother's face with a thinly wicked grin.

"She must be some lovebird, that big Polack. Worth it?"

"Shut up."

Cullin chuckled and went out.

Raven glanced at the mirror to confirm that his face was really as swiss-steaked as it felt. She was a strong woman, and he hadn't blocked all her blows. His nose was bleeding, his lip split, and if his right eye wasn't swollen wholly shut by morning, it would be damned funny.

He returned to the common room and dropped the cutlery he had collected in the corner. "That's all, I reckon."

"Now we'll see to Billy's leg. You." Shallot gave Anna a curt nod. "Get some clean cloth."

"I do nothing," she said quietly. "You dirt. I no do for any of you. All of you, dirt."

A nerve-flick of temper touched Shallot's gaunt jaw. "Well enough. But you'll —"

"I will." Aimee Parnell stood up timidly. "I have a clean dress, an old one. I will tear it up."

Her husband rose too, looking waxy around the lips. "I can help," he said nervously.

Shallot barked a laugh. "Ah, yes — the Spartan spirit of the Christian vanguard. And what will you do, sir? Hold his hand and roll bandages?"

"Take out the shot, treat him, make him as comfortable as possible."

"What the hell do you know about doctoring?"

"Enough." Parnell managed a determined nod. "I'll want a pint or so of that rotgut from the bar. And a man to hold him."

Shallot tugged his lower lip. "Sounds all right. Go in there with them, Milt."

They entered the annex.

It was a long-abandoned stable that Cernak had slightly renovated by tearing out stalls, patching the walls, and throwing up an eighteen-foot covered passageway to connect the old building with the roadhouse. The single room was partitioned down the center by a heavy brocaded drapery of some faded material, doubtless scavenged from one of the old buildings. The log walls were lined with the crudest sort of double bunks.

Mendez' swarthy face was the color of dirty paste under the overhead coal oil lamp. He was in obvious agony. He tried to grin at them. "Me," he whispered, "Billy Mendez, the son of hidalgoes. Is this a way to die?"

Parnell glanced at Raven, who shrugged. "Fancy of his. Always claims he's the bastard son of some big don in Sonora."

"Is not fancy, amigo."

Aimee came from behind the drapery,

carrying a clean, long-faded frock. She began tearing it into strips with an efficient vigor, her small face purposeful, a black curl lopping down on her forehead.

Parnell carefully tugged free the dirty bandanna tied around Mendez' leg. The blood had started to clot; the Mexican jerked and groaned.

"Easy," Parnell murmured. "Easy now, boy. I just want a look . . ."

There was a smoothly half-absent professionalism in his tone; his whole attention was on the bloody wound as he slowly exposed it. *A preacher,* Raven thought. *I wonder.*

"There is nothing but to dig out some shot," Aimee said tonelessly. "Even for you, James, this should be an easy operation."

Parnell faintly reddened. "Thanks for the pleasantry. Come have a look."

She did. A small gasp hissed from her, and she swallowed with an effort.

"Exactly," Parnell said. "I'll want some boiling water and those tiny silver tweezers of yours." He glanced at Raven. "Would you have a jackknife?"

Raven dug it out and handed it to him. Aimee went out very quickly. Mendez twisted on the bunk, his face sweat-shining and softly contorted.

"Lie still."

"Sure, Doc, sure. But sweet Maria, this is a bitch with all her claws in. What about it, Doc, eh, the leg?"

"I'm not a doctor," Parnell said mechanically. "I'm a minister of the gospel."

"Okay, Padre. Okay. But you fix her up, yes?"

Shallot came in with a large tin cup of Cernak's pale liquor, which Mendez seized and drank as if it were water.

"H'm — h'm." Shallot peered closely at the wound. "Opened him up like a gutted steer, didn't it? Think you can save this mess?"

Mendez lowered the cup, the whites of his eyes showing. "Nobody take off my leg."

Parnell sent Shallot an irritated glance. "Easy, son. Let's clean it up before making conclusions."

Aimee returned with the hot water. Parnell dipped the tweezers and began pulling shreds of underwear cloth from the mangled flesh. Mendez jerked and shuddered.

"Hold still, boy." Parnell looked sharply at Raven. "Hold his ankles, will you?"

Raven gripped the wounded man's legs and leaned his weight. Parnell used the small jackknife blade to dig for the shot. Mendez whimpered and violently twisted his torso. He gave several thin screams.

61

With the tweezers, Parnell clattered the pellets one by one into a bowl. His face was calm, but Raven saw his lips twitch every time the Mexican screamed.

Afterward he washed the pulped red flesh and made a painful examination. "Easy . . ." Mendez released a long shriek, his body writhing so violently that even Shallot was moved to help, pinning Mendez above the chest.

The minister looked up, his face pale and shining. "The kneecap is . . . well, it's . . ."

Mendez reared up on his elbows. "You fix her, Padre, the leg."

"Well . . ." Parnell avoided his eyes and picked up a cloth strip. "We'll bandage it now and have a look in the morning."

Raven stared at him. He knew little about doctoring, but he had seen smashed joints of knees or elbows before this. Maybe a big-city medico could save the limb after a fashion. But in a backwoods camp, there was only one sensible answer.

Parnell knew it, too. His face, as he applied the dressing, looked as if he were about to be sick.

Shallot gave him a cat-with-mouse study, laughing silently. "Want a drink, Dominie?" His noiseless chuckles dissolved in a coughing fit, a bad one. He was half doubled, holding his chest and gasping, as he staggered from the annex.

Parnell said, "Consumptive?"

Raven shrugged. "Finish up and we'll get back with the others."

"I will stay here," Aimee said, laying a flat, warm compress on Mendez' brow. "There should be someone to watch."

Mendez giggled worriedly, following every movement of Parnell's hands. "Ah, sweet lady. You will start, yes, by giving me more booze?"

Raven and the minister returned to the common room. As they entered, Anna Kosciusko was speaking to her father with a low, vibrant force — that foreign tongue again. She stopped to glare at Raven. She was sitting on the bench, holding her little boy close.

Shallot was huddled over the plank bar, putting down a massive slug of white mule. He took another. Spots of color burned in his wan cheeks. Everyone was watching him.

He straightened finally. "All right. Let's all be comfortable." He shrugged off his mackinaw and tossed it over the bar. He seemed slight to frailty in a rough-knit turtleneck sweater and a corduroy coat.

He moved to the center of the room, rubbing his thin hands together. "Let's get down to cases. Polack, you know what we want. Only question before the house is, how hard will you make it?"

Cernak sat with his head sunk between his shoulders, elbows resting on his knees. He did not answer.

Albie gave a fevered honk of laughter. "Let me burn 'im, Cap'n George. Let me burn 'im a little."

"Albie," Shallot said gently, "shut up."

Cernak raised his shaggy head. He nodded at the fire, whose flames had been stoked to a high, ruddy dance. "I already laid your fire for you. Get started with it."

Shallot squared away before him, hands on hips. The skull-grin rested light as thistledown on his lips. "That could happen. But not necessarily to you, Polack. Think a little."

Cernak's head jerked barely sideways. But he caught himself before looking at his daughter and grandson. His chin slowly dropped till his eyes rested on a point between his feet.

"You're wasting time," Shallot murmured, and motioned brusquely. "Albie, get out your gun."

Albie obeyed, snickering, and when

Shallot said, "Cover Quintus and Milt," he did so at once.

"George," Terrill said, blinking, "what the devil!"

Raven, guessing Shallot's intent as purely as Terrill had missed it, had started a movement toward his gun. But his coat was still on; he had to fumble.

Then Dolph, who already had his pistol out to cover the room at large, swung it on him. "Man, you want to get a bullet in your brisket, you better make sure it's worth the game."

"What'n hell!" Cullin said.

"Your brother and Quintus won't have belly for this," Shallot said patiently, "I don't want them interfering."

"Yeah?" Cullin began to grin.

"One moment," Shallot said, and looked at Anna. "Perhaps *you* can tell us."

"Tell you what?" Her dark eyes flared sullenly. "I not know what you want! I never see you."

"True. Perhaps you saw the money, though."

"What money? What you mean?"

"I'll explain, then. Your daddy —"

"Shallot." Cernak raised his head, flame-eyed. He held out his big hands, opening and closing the fingers. "Don't tell her. Or

I will kill you. With these hands, I twist off your head."

Shallot made a quick, almost imperceptible motion. A gun appeared in his fist. "You'll try, let's say. But you'll never make it off that bench. I promise you."

Cernak's deep-set eyes smoldered.

"A thousand miles south of here," Shallot said, addressing Anna, "in a big state, Texas, is a little town called Baileyville. In that town is a bank that seasonally bulges with cattle-sale money. Last fall — a little over a year ago — we decided to take that money. We planned the operation for weeks. Six of us. Me, Quintus, Dolph Smith, Billy Mendez, Albie, and a Polack we all knew as Rolvinski."

"Shallot," — a half-plea rumbled in Cernak's tone now — "don't tell her this. I ask you."

"Well," Shallot went on conversationally, "we took it, all right. But somebody had tipped off the law. As we came out of the bank, armed townsmen poured from buildings like hornets from a nest. It was a clumsily set ambush, but I did take a bullet through the chest" — he coughed lightly — "and then we scattered. We'd agreed on a later rendezvous, should anything go awry. And we all met there. All but one. The one who was carrying the sack of loot when we ran from the bank. He never showed up. And we never saw him again — till tonight."

Anna slid a bewildered glance to her father, then back to Shallot. "What is it you say?" she whispered.

"Let's not get ahead of our story, m'dear. We laid low for a long spell, till the hue and cry quieted down. Then we put out cautious feelers. It was just possible, of course, that something had happened to our friend. He might have taken a bullet during the escape and died on the prairie. But time had passed; we'd heard nothing — as would be the case if his remains had turned up. Our old pal Rudy Rolvinski had plain dropped out of sight.

"We kept our ears to the grapevine. We all had friends; our friends had friends. If the Polack got in touch with anyone we knew — if he began to spend the money . . .

"Finally a chance word — a stroke of pure luck. A friend's friend who knew our story had come over the pass here and stopped at this station. It was, he reported, run by a Pole named Anton Cernak who had a suspicious air about him, was the right age, etcetera. The only hitch — he seemed to be a staid family man, a widower living with his daughter and grandson — not a footloose loner as Rolvinski had been.

"Luckily the friend's friend asked questions of others. Learned that Cernak had bought the station only this spring — an out-at-the-heels drifter who plunked down an incredible wad of greenbacks in payment. Not too long afterward he was joined by the daughter and grandson."

Shallot smiled. "Ideal, d'you see? A remote roadhouse in the mountains, a thousand miles from Baileyville — and you and your son helping to fill out his cover. At the same time, as proprietor of a swing station, he was serving a purpose, not just mysteriously living here. Arousing no suspicion, attracting no attention, waiting till both the law and his old friends tired of looking for him."

Her eyes were tinged with a faint sickness. "Papa? This is so?"

Cernak heaved a growl from the depth of his chest. "It's so. But I don't have the money."

"Ah-ah." Shallot waggled a finger at him. "Honor bright, Polack. Lying low all that while, you could hardly have spent it. This rundown station didn't set you back much. Even getting the daughter and grandchild out of Europe couldn't have dented you over a couple of thousand."

Cernak hesitated perceptibly. "Don't mean I spent it all. It's in a bank in, eh, the East."

"What bank? Where?"

"Philadelphia."

"The bank's name?"

"I forget."

Shallot hiked his hip over the corner of the table, folded his arms, and eyed Cernak with the thin, intent smile of a kid de-winging a fly. "Polack," he said pleasantly, "that's a plate of cowshit soup if I've heard one. That surly, suspicious old-country peasant type of which you are a prime example doesn't trust banks even when his money isn't stolen."

He looked again at Anna. "You haven't an idea where it might be, eh?"

"If I know, I tell you. My son and me, *we* no need this dirty money."

"I believe you. Playtime's over, then." Shallot stood and pointed with his gun at the turkey trot. "Albie, take this lady into that annex and keep her there. If she gives you trouble, hit her. But lightly."

Albie blinked his understanding and walked to the bench. "Get up, lady."

"No," Anna said.

He gave his gun a menacing swipe at her head. Reluctantly she stood and picked up Laddie.

"I forgot," Shallot said softly. "The boy stays here."

She looked at him with a slow, agonized disbelief, which faded to terror. "No! You no touch him."

Terrill still couldn't believe it. "George, do I understand —"

"Just shut your jaw, Quintus," Shallot said wearily. "Albie, take the boy away."

Grinning, Albie sheathed his gun and laid hold of the little boy's shoulders. Anna screamed a foreign word and let go at Albie with a clenched fist. He howled as she caught him in the eye.

His prompt comeback of a hamlike fist smacked her flush on the jaw. She slipped to the floor without a sound.

Cernak surged to his feet.

"Sit down, Polack!" Shallot cocked his pistol. "I'll drop you, by God!"

Cernak swung his head bearlike, his small eyes red-hot with fury. His weight was sprung onto the balls of his feet. At last he settled back on his heels, defeated.

Albie had seized up the kicking, squirming boy, and now Shallot went to the nearest fireplace and picked up a blackened poker. He walked to the boy, who had stopped fighting against the grip of Albie's arms, clamped around his torso and legs.

Shallot reached out to lightly flick the boy's cheek with the poker tip. A charcoal streak sprang across the tender flesh.

"Not even a blister," Shallot murmured. "But suppose, now, that it had been heated in those coals about five minutes. Even a touch like that . . ."

Cernak had sunk back on the bench. He sat bolt upright, clenched fists resting on his knees. His eyes held an unfocused glare. Sweat poured down the crease of his jaw.

"Oh, my God," Terrill whispered. "George, for the love of —"

"Quintus, *shut up!*"

Shallot half snarled the words as he wheeled now and tramped back to the fireplace. He plunged the poker into the red heap of coals.

Raven held his weight balanced forward, ready to seize the first chance. But a glance at Dolph Smith told him there would be none. Dolph's face was stone-still, the eyes veiled and watchful. However the situation touched him personally (most likely he didn't give a damn), he would take Shallot's orders.

A wrong move and he was as good as dead, Raven knew. Dolph's ungainly build was deceptive. When he chose to move fast, he was supremely graceful, quick as a snake.

The firelight played on Shallot's wasted features and on his fleshless smile that was meaningless now. *There's your answer,* Raven thought. Even Shallot's best and oldest friend, Terrill, could no longer sway him.

Crazy? It was hard to say. As hard as it was to say about Cullin. But there was something wrong in both of them.

Glancing at his brother now, Raven saw the hard shiny glaze on his eyes as he watched Shallot lift out the poker and drive its tip lightly against the floor. The puncheon smoked wispily; a spot of char grew.

Cernak stared like a mesmerized bear, his eyes never leaving the poker as Shallot carried it across the room.

James Parnell watched too, white as death. But he made no movement, nor the faintest sound. Funny, these preachers. They talked of a fire-and-brimstone devil that nobody ever saw anymore, but show them one in the flesh and they couldn't believe he really was.

Shallot said, "Anytime, Polack," and lowered the poker till it was an inch from the boy's leg.

Faint chugging noises rasped in Cernak's throat.

Little Laddie Kosciusko did not show a flicker of fear. He watched the iron unblinkingly. Even when it touched his long nightshirt and the cloth smoldered and blackened, he made only a faint sound.

Shallot's lips were drawn off his teeth. His face held the damnedest expression: not lust, but a peculiar dreamy fascination. Sweat sheened the puckered lines bracketing his mouth.

The boy must have felt the heat; he squirmed against Albie's hold.

Raven let his muscles bunch loosely, gathering for a leap. The hell with Dolph's gun; the hell with everything. He wasn't letting this happen.

"I'll tell. I'll tell."

The words left Cernak in a kind of guttural explosion. Shallot took the poker away slowly . . . slowly. His expression faded back to a bony blandness.

"Well, fine, Polack," he said, and carelessly tossed the poker into a corner. "That's fine."

5

Anna Kosciusko sat on the bench and hugged Laddie tightly to her. There was a numb agony in the pit of her stomach. She could not stop trembling. She did not know all that had happened while she was unconscious; she could not bring herself to ask. She had seen the charred spot on her son's nightshirt. That was enough. Again and again she had examined the skin of his leg to assure herself there was no pink sign of a burn. Over and over again she had made him tell her that he was not hurt.

Anna held him tighter. She hardly thought of her own life anymore. Life for her had ended three years ago on the blood-splashed cobbles of a street in Warsaw. Only small Ladislas mattered now. Her son. And Stephen's.

She stared at Captain George Shallot. He made her think of a snake. What kind of a man could do such a thing? What kind were these others that they would let him?

One after another Anna studied the men. She had seen that the big fair one called Quintus was different from the rest. And so (she had been shocked to realize) was Milt Raven. He was the last of whom she would have expected a decent feeling. Yet Shallot had ordered him held at gunpoint, too.

She still felt fear of the big man. She couldn't help it. That face had stayed branded on her memory through a thousand nightmares. Even though she had never seen Milt Raven until a few hours ago.

Her father was talking in a slurred mutter. ". . . so I hid it way up there. An old mineshaft on the Corona claim."

"How far?" Shallot snapped.

"Maybe four mile up. There is only the one trail. It's too narrow for a wagon. They used to pack the bullion down muleback, I heard. All this snow now . . . I don't think a horse can climb it."

"Men with snowshoes can. I noticed you have three pairs in your loft. We'll start out first light tomorrow. That's if the storm quits. If it hasn't, we'll lay in here for as long as necessary."

"One thing I better know first." Cernak's

eyes flickered with red lights. "When you got the money, what happens?"

Shallot seemed surprised. "Why, not a thing . . . to any of you. Why should it? All we came for was the loot."

Cernak grunted. "So I trust you, eh?"

Shallot smiled. "Of course not. You trust Quintus. You know him, Polack. You know he'll see to it that any bargain I make is kept."

Terrill gave him a bitter stare. Shallot laughed and pivoted on his heel. He walked to the bar and poured a jolt of white mule into a cup. He took a long drink and smiled at the whole room. His cheeks flamed; his eyes cooled.

"Ahhh . . . Folks, let's try not to make the occasion more unbearable than necessary. My boys will bunk in the annex. The women and the little boy can share that room off the kitchen. The preacher, the Polack, and the Irish son of Jehu will be ensconced in the loft. I want the latter two tied up. The rest have the freedom of the house so long as they behave themselves."

Dolph scowled. "Man, you letting 'em all wander about?"

"Two women, a little boy, and he of the cloth?" Shallot chuckled dyspeptically. "They're about equally harmless. The preacher'll have to see after Billy; the women will make our meals. Meantime we have all the weapons here — and I think nobody's fool enough to try an escape in this weather. I want two men up and awake at all times. One will stay on guard down here, another in the loft. You can choose up duty any way you like. Oh — and gentlemen, you'll all leave the women alone."

He said it half-absently — an afterthought. As if the matter really were of no concern. He tilted the cup to his lips, drained it. Suddenly he spat the liquor out. He doubled up in a coughing fit.

When he straightened again, his eyes were dangerous. "Polack, I want your good whiskey. Where is it?"

Cernak gestured surlily toward the bar.

"I don't mean this slop," Shallot snarled. "You always fancied a good drink. You have a private bottle around somewhere. Better produce it. Or by God I'll find it, and when I do —"

"I get it," Anna said in a chilly voice. "Is in the kitchen."

Shallot said narrowly, "Cooperation all at once? Why?"

"I'll keep a watch on her," Cullin grinned.

Watch her! He had done little else. Anna walked ahead of him to the kitchen, where a single candle fluttered on the sinkboard. Her walk was a little unsteady; she was still dizzy from Albie's blow. The whole side of her face was a raw, throbbing ache.

She pulled a chair over to the sinkboard and stood on it. As she reached to the top shelf for Anton's bottle of good Irish whiskey, she glanced between two canisters on the middle shelf and saw the soft wink of steel. Good. That was the small knife she used for peeling potatoes. It had taken Laddie's fancy and he was always playing with it. Finally she had stowed it out of his reach. As she'd expected, it had escaped Raven's notice when he searched the kitchen. Later she would transfer it to her apron pocket.

Anna stepped down and replaced the chair. Cullin's stare, following her movements, made her flesh crawl. Even in the sacklike nightgown she felt exposed.

She was used to looks from male stage passengers. It was a lonely country, men still outnumbered women four to one, some went for months without seeing a woman. She did not mind them looking their fill. For any that wanted more, she had a work-hardened hand that, laid flat across a man's jaw, made a discouraging argument.

But she'd never seen such unabashed lust as in this Cullin's face — and she had seen plenty of it, here and in the old country. Uneasy as she felt, she didn't fear him as she did his great brute of a brother, who was only indifferent.

He blocked the door. "You no stand my way," she said coldly.

He moved slightly. Anna had to turn sideways to go out past him. The peak of one breast grazed his arm. His chuckle was pitched for her ears alone.

Shallot was leaning on the bar. Anna set the bottle down, but kept her hand closed firmly around it. "I want talk to my father," she said stonily. "Alone."

Shallot took hold of the bottle, and she tightened her hand. He was unmoving for a moment, his eyes turning softly vicious. He yanked the bottle away, threw out the remaining liquor in his cup, and filled it to the brim with the good brandy. He drank off half of it, closed his eyes, and rolled his tongue over his lips.

He looked squarely at her. If he touched her, Anna thought, it would be like a snake's touch. But she didn't think he would try. He did not look as if a woman would do him much good.

"Imagine you and Daddy do have a few

thoughts to thrash out." His tone was sardonic, amused, almost genial now. "Sit over at the table."

Anna walked to the bench where her father was slumped with head down, arms loose, and fingers splayed on his thighs. He resembled a tired ape.

"Now we talk," she said.

The surly-bear look flickered on Cernak's face, but it vanished. He nodded heavily. "I guess it's time for that."

Anna turned to Aimee Parnell. "You will take my little boy, please, to our room?"

Aimee nodded mutely. She took Laddie's hand, and he went willingly with her.

Anna and her father sat at the trestle table, facing each other across it. In Polish she said, low-voiced, "This sick little man says you helped steal money. Then you betrayed him and these others so you could have it all. This, you say, is all true."

"I did it for you, sister. For the boy."

"For us! You say this? You have not even acted like you want us! I've wondered again and again — why did you send for us?"

Anton's brows pulled down like shaggy veils. "I know I haven't been gentle. A man forgets how to be. But I wanted you. A man gets to know how lonely he is. That was when I wrote to Stanislaus. And he wrote back that your husband was dead and you needed help."

"So you used stolen money to bring us here."

Cernak scowled. "Do you know why I left Poland?"

"I know what Uncle Stanislaus always told. That when the people tried to drive the Russians from our country — the revolt of eighteen sixty-three — you were connected with a revolutionary group. That when the revolt failed, you fled Warsaw."

"True," Cernak said harshly. "But there was more. The authorities seized our group. All but me, I escaped. We had money hidden against an emergency. My friends were imprisoned, sentenced to death. I was sent word to get the money into the right hands so that my friends could be freed." He began to rub his hand over his brow as though it ached intolerably.

"And?"

"I got the money. Then I turned scared. Instead I used it to get out of the country . . . turned my back on everything I had believed — on the people who believed in me. I came to this country. In those days there was a civil war going on here. I went to Madison, Wisconsin, and enlisted in a regiment made up of Polish immigrants. I thought if I could fight for them — my own people in a new country — it would make up . . ."

His voice trailed.

"Go on," she said coldly. "You have started this."

"Ah," he said wearily. "After this civil war there was a thing called a Homestead Act. A man could get so much land free, a hundred and sixty acres. I married again. I farmed in Minnesota. Wheat. But it was one thing and then another. Locusts, drought, hail. My wife died. That was the end, and I went west and rammed around at different things. They were . . . most of them were not good things.

"A couple years ago I met this Shallot and his bunch. We did a few jobs together. We stole cattle in Williamson County, Texas, and ran them down on night drives to the Gulf Coast and a crooked buyer. We saw this bank and it looked like an easy job. Shallot has told you the rest."

Anna sat looking down at her hands folded on the table. She was torn several ways and did not know what to feel. This man was her blood father, yet she did not know him at all.

82

She had been only four years old when he had fled Warsaw, leaving her with his brother's family. That much they had told her, but she had no memory of him. She did have a treasured ambrotype of the two of them together. A small girl and her big, youthful father, she serious, he grinning into the camera like an overgrown bear cub. Her mother, she was told, had died in bearing her.

Twenty-one years had passed, during which she had grown to womanhood, married Stephen Kosciusko, and borne a child of her own, while she had learned year by year the bitter yoke of a conquered, broken people. She had watched her impatient, fiery young husband help spark a street riot against the oppressions of the regime. And she had seen him cut down before her eyes.

Her life for the next two years had been a living nightmare. Then one night a knock on the door, a whispered message. Be at a certain place on a certain evening, said her caller, if you wish to get out of Poland with your son.

At first she had been suspicious. A trap by the authorities? Yet she knew, as did all Poles, of a secret organization that would arrange expatriation for a price. The palms of petty officialdom must be greased, the hidden gears kept oiled.

 Nothing could be worse than continuing as she was. She would take the chance.

Two men were waiting at the place. Her father's money, she was told, had arranged everything, and soon she would join him in America. The rest was a chimera of vagrant impressions. You walked and walked and walked. In all kinds of weather. Across all kinds of country. For a week of nights and days. Brief halts for meals and sleep, but only by day. At an obscure Balkan port you were rowed under cover of darkness out to an ancient clipper ship. For six weeks you huddled miserably in a foul and crowded steerage, hugging your child for warmth and comfort, hardly able to gag down the rancid food brought you. Ahead of you a strange land, an unknown destination.

Yet you were oddly buoyed. The darkest moments were cheered by thoughts of a big man with clear, honest eyes and laughter on his lips. A man who had given all but his life for his country and would have given that if it could have helped. A man who had left his daughter the most precious legacy of all.

Whenever you exhorted your young son

to remember his hero father, you told him of an equally brave grandfather.

Now you could tell him that his grandfather was alive and well in a new land. Not dead, as all had believed. And they would see him soon.

The trip by train and stage across the lush, rolling farmlands and awesome plains of a continent had been like an epic journey.

But at its end she had found only a remote, deserted town, a gruff, taciturn man whose spirit was a desiccated echo of all she had held her father to be.

She had tried to make allowances. What business did she have holding on like a miser to a girlish idolatry of a father she could not remember? But there was a germ of self-deception in that thought too, she had realized. The smiling youth in the ambrotype and this crabby unapproachable stranger were the same man. He had drastically changed, that was all.

Anna's standards were hard ones. They had been fired in a bitter crucible. What if life had treated him shabbily? It had been so with others. Men who had not betrayed their comrades even under torture, who had not let fear or privation drive them to sniveling thievery.

His chair creaked as his weight came forward. "Do you hate me now, sister?"

"No. You are my father. I will never hate you."

Anton did not miss the cold qualifying finality in her tone. "Then, what is it you can't forgive? Tell me."

"I can tell you," she said. "But it's a thing of honor, so you won't understand. After Stephen's death, it was very bad for us. My husband was an enemy of the state — a dangerous man. It wasn't enough that his widow and boy grieved, that we never had food or fuel in the house, that we had to beg from neighbors. Every way they could — short of arrest and torture — they persecuted us. Our house was watched. No matter where I went, I was followed — by three or four of them. Every night the Russian officers came drunk to my door and beat on it and said things . . . things that my son could hear. When I did not give in to them, it got worse.

"But I had one thing, Papa. Call it pride, call it honor. It kept me alive — resisting. It was built on what my husband had been and what I believed my father was. With Stephen anyway, it was real. But it began with you. Now that part is nothing."

The sandy tufts of his brows drew together. "So you blame me —"

"Not for that. I made my own picture of my father. That lie was my doing. No. I think I blame you for destroying the lie. It was a good lie, about decency and honor. Always I've taught my son the pride of doing right. How do I tell him now that his honored grandfather is a thief?"

"Why do you give the thing such a twist?" Cernak growled. "The money! My God, you think I don't remember how it was in the old country? Or what it's like to be alone and penniless in a new country? That's what Laddie might never have had to know, thanks to that dirty money!"

"Here?"

"Of course not here! We'd have stayed at this place just a few years, till all had cooled down. Then a nice farm or ranch . . . schooling for the boy . . . a fine life for all of us."

"But now there will not be a nice farm or fine schools, will there?"

Anna pushed back her chair and rose. She saw the lines of old suffering that troughed his heavy face. She wanted to feel pity. But she could not.

"That fat one knocked me out, so I don't know . . . maybe you'll tell me. I know it wasn't easy for you to say where the money was. I know this because my son's night-shirt has a burn. But now I wonder how long it took? How long before you decided not to let them torture your grandson?"

"Christ," Cernak said. "Christ, Anna."

"Maybe it's in Him to forgive you, Papa. Don't ask me again why I can't."

6

It was cold in the annex. Wind slashed through an unstopped chink and guttered the table candle. Quintus Terrill sat on the edge of a bunk, wearily working off his left boot — a laborious chore for a one-armed man. When he had the boot off, he only sat and dully stared at it in his hand. Albie was already snoring in another bunk. Shallot was still out in the common room, and the two Ravens had agreed to take the first guard duty — Milt on the ground floor, Cullin in the loft. Dolph Smith and Billy Mendez were in their bunks on the other side of the drapery. Billy, though numbed by vast slugs of whiskey, was sawing out intermittent groans of pain.

Terrill had not believed he'd held onto any illusions after all these years. Give Shallot that much — he always tried to avoid killing. Sometimes, in their different escapades, people get hurt. But a man could get shot any number of places without dying at once. If some died later, you never heard about it.

Funny too. Of jobs they had done, this one had seemed the least likely to involve gunplay. You sent two men ahead to scout the ground, then laid your plans logically. It was the illogic of a half-witted stockboy who had elected to spend a winter night in a cold stable that had proved their undoing. And the boy's own. God, yes.

But the little boy. That was the worst.

Tramp of boots in the dog trot. Shallot came in, walking unsteadily. He crossed to the bunk adjoining Quintus', dropped onto it with a grunt, and held out the bottle.

"No," Terrill said.

"No need to ask," Shallot said dryly. "Your face says it all. All right, Quintus, get it out."

"Would you have burned that little boy, George?"

Shallot said, "Ahhh!" with a fathomless disgust. "For hell's sake, Quintus, how many times did you burn yourself when you were a kid?"

"I don't know," Terrill said woodenly. "I just don't recall one grown man holding me down while another applied a hot poker."

"For Christ's sake, man! We got what we were after and we didn't have to burn him! Anyhow, a little burn. However he gets it, what's a little burn to a kid?"

"And if a little burn hadn't turned the trick? My God, George. Torturing a little boy. What's happened to you? To us?"

"Well, I'm Joe-be-damned." He swung to his feet and rubbed the back of his neck, staring at his lieutenant. "Is it possible, after all these years, that you still believe you're on an itinerant tea party with Robin Hood and his Merrie Men? You wear that goddam Southern knight's code in your head like it was something God Almighty handed you on a stone tablet."

From the other side of the drape, Dolph snapped, "Would you *gents* mind terribly shutting up so's us colored people can get some sleep?"

Shallot swung on his heel, staring at the curtain. "I can remember when a darkie talked like that, he got his wick trimmed goddam fast."

Terrill stuck his foot back in his boot and yanked it on. "Why don't you just shoot him? You should find it easy as stepping on a fly."

He got up and walked to the turkey trot. "Where are you going?"

91

"To get a drink."

Shallot raised the brandy bottle. "Here's a drink, a good one. Of course if you prefer slop —"

"Slop suits the other pigs," Terrill said. "It suits me. It should you."

Shallot nodded amusedly. "You're in a mood, old pal. It'll last the night anyhow."

Terrill went out to the common room. It was deserted except for Raven, slouched in a chair by one of the fireplaces. Terrill stepped behind the bar and sloshed liquor into a cup.

He drank deeply of the potent stuff, so deeply it made his eyes water. The fumes mounted dizzily to his head, loosening the fabric of his thoughts; they fell apart in bitter ravels.

He drained his cup and drank again. He stared at the gilded chandelier. Watching the leap of rosy flames polish its gaudy facets with a multitude of rainbow shimmers . . .

Anther chandelier long ago, all silver and crystal. A white-pillared mansion and liveried servants and a genteel mother. Best of schools? Of course. And a girl who had promised to wait.

Funny. All the boys in their "set" had been big, handsome, strapping fellows —

all but skinny little George Shallot, "The Runt." Yet George was the leader on every crazy lark, flailing the rest of them with that bright mad intensity of his. He'd had a way of looking, of smiling, of bringing things off with a certain flair. He'd needed those attributes. Nature had gifted his friends physically. They'd had nothing to prove. He, everything.

At some point that easy flair had degenerated into a pure meanness. It had come so imperceptibly that Quintus had accepted it in small grudging doses. A man got immunized. Or was *addicted* the word?

The war. That was funny, too. It had started out as the biggest lark of all. An irregular regiment composed of young dandies from the best families, not one of them above eighteen, riding out to defend Virginia, the Confederacy, and woman's honor. Led by young Captain George.

Four years later a broken, ragged handful remained. Outlawed for guerrilla terrorism, refused amnesty, they had struck west. Texas, California, Mexico.

Now only he and Shallot were left.

Honest work? Of course. Numerous attempts anyhow. Everything from bookkeeping to swamping stables. One trouble was that a lot of people wouldn't hire a one-armed man. Another trouble was his own core of fiery pride that would accept only so much menial work.

But mostly, he supposed, it was his phenomenal capacity for self-delusion. For each wrong turn, a man forged an illusion to go with it. And when he looked back and made his excuses, he looked only at the events he couldn't have controlled, never those he might have and hadn't even tried controlling.. Yep. That was the real trick, all right.

Terrill was drinking steadily. And getting quite drunk. But as he knew by now, there were worse ways to be. Such as sober and thinking. He filled the cup again.

The first thing Anna did when she returned to her room was to change to her everyday clothes. She did not feel easy in a nightgown — not while she had to share a roof with those men. She would sleep with her clothes on, and she advised Aimee Parnell to do the same.

The minister's wife sat on the edge of the bed, her young face pallid. Suddenly she burst into tears.

Laddie sat up in the bedclothes, gazing at her with distress. "Little Mother, the pretty lady is crying."

"Hush." Anna spoke in Russian, too — the hated tongue that both knew better than English or their native Polish. "Go to sleep, my son."

She sat beside Aimee and put an arm around her. "No cry. It do no good."

"I can't help it. I'm afraid. But I am selfish; I think only of me. Look at your poor face! You are so brave, Anna."

Anna had already looked at her poor face, in the tarnished mirror over her commode. Her whole right jaw was gently ballooning and turning livid. She wondered how it would look by morning. Maybe she could relieve the ache and hold the swelling down with some snow.

She had been too angry to be afraid, but she was starting to feel afraid. Maybe they had come for the money and nobody would be hurt if they got it. But she was far from sure. That Cullin was a personal worry to her. And Shallot. The man must be a little crazy. How could you guess what a man like that might do next?

Gabe. They had killed Gabe; what did they have to lose now? Poor loose-witted Gabe, who had loved the horses that were his special charge. So many times on so many nights he had left his warm bed in the loft to sleep out in the stable with his big, ugly shotgun. Sometimes he would ask Anton to bar the door outside and lock him in. Who would have thought that that innocent habit would cost his life?

"No worry," she said, patting Aimee's shoulder. "They get their money, soon be gone. Now you lay down. Both go sleep."

She went back through the kitchen to the common room.

At the bar Quintus Terrill was drinking and staring fixedly at the chandelier. Milt Raven was slacked in a chair by the east fireplace, his legs crossed.

Ignoring them both, Anna went to the nearest window and unbarred the shutters across it. The common room windows were the only ones that could be opened.

"What're you doing?"

Raven's voice was toneless and incurious. The crumbling fire had dimmed to red glimmers. With the flicker of ebbing firelight on his rock-hewn features he looked like a great, brutish animal who might spring anytime. Anna noted with satisfaction the small damage that her fists had done to his face.

"I get snow," she snapped, and opened the shutters, then the windows, and quickly scooped a handful off the sill. She closed the window and shutters and stood glaring at him as she held the snow to her sore cheek.

He said nothing. She stared at his face, feeling her jaws tighten with hatred.

Again she saw the Russian cavalry officer rising in his stirrups, his prey-bird's face distorted with pleasure. His saber flashing and falling. Stephen dropping in the street, his blood showering the cobbles.

This Raven was a much bigger man than the officer who had killed her husband. And younger. But add ten years to his face, and the European cavalryman's coveted saber scar — the likeness was uncanny.

Anna whirled about and strode back to her room.

Her fist had closed so tightly on the snow that only an icy lump remained. She pressed it to her hot face and stared at her image in the mirror. Ordinarily her brown eyes were exactly like Laddie's — quick and friendly and curious. Now the look in them shocked her.

Aimee and Laddie lay quietly, watching her. Anna blew out the candle and lay down on her son's other side, and pulled the covers to her chin.

That man. Raven. Why did he have to come with his evil-bird face and bring it all back as it had been? She had begun to accept that her old life was done, that she must start anew in a new country. Now the struggle to forget, to shape a newness in her mind, must begin all over.

Laddie snugged close to her in the dark. "Little Mother," he whispered, "these are very bad men."

"Yes, my son."

"If I had a gun," he said judiciously, "I would shoot them all."

Pride welled into her throat, warm and tight. How like Stephen he was! She had often been afraid for Stephen because he'd been afraid of nothing. She'd been right . . .

The howl of wind deepened. A skirling blast of snow buffeted the house; again the logs trembled. *Stephen*, her mind cried silently, *Stephen* . . .

Half-torn scars bled in her mind. It was a long time before she found sleep. When it came, her tired mind grabbed gratefully at its refuge.

7

Before morning Mendez was in such pain that his screams aroused everybody. Nobody had been sleeping well anyway, unless it were little Laddie Kosciusko. He went promptly back to sleep. The others came out to the common room. Even Cernak and O'Herlihy were untied, brought down from the loft, and permitted a drink apiece. The Reverend Mr. Parnell tried to feed Mendez more whiskey, but he was able to take only a little. In a few minutes he had thrown it up.

Shallot seemed amused. "You can't keep him drunk forever, Dominie. You know that leg's got to come off."

Parnell sat slumped at the table. He looked up, his face haggard. "I'm no surgeon — no physician."

Shallot gave him a long, speculative stare but didn't pursue the matter. He dug a chunky Waltham watch from his pocket.

"Half an hour or so to first daylight. I'll

take a look at the weather. Wind seems to have slackened off. Come on, Albie."

He got up and went to an antler rack mounted by the door and took down his mackinaw. Shrugging into it, he glanced at Anna. "You," he said curtly, "make us some breakfast. Coffee first."

Albie had lumbered over to lift the crossbar from the door, and now he threw on his coat and hurried out after his chief.

Anna rose from the table and walked out to the kitchen, Cullin's gaze following her. Maybe more intensely than usual, since he too had begun pulling at the raw whiskey. All of them were, except Raven and Dolph.

The gaunt Negro huddled in a chair close to the fire, a blanket around him and his long grasshopper legs doubled up under him. The cold had got into his joints and had him in an uglier mood than usual.

Aimee Parnell timidly broke the silence. "Last night, Mr. O'Herlihy, you mention a white owl. I am most curious. I have never heard of such a thing."

Her husband glanced up. "I think . . . once I did. From an old hired man when I was a small boy in Maine."

O'Herlihy was rubbing his thick wrists where the ropes had chafed them raw.

"Aye, they're real enough. Up in Northern Canada, I hear, past the Arctic circle. I'd hazard that an Arctic owl this far south means as cruel a winter as this country's seen."

"You sure?" Cernak rumbled. "One five years ago was bad enough."

"Pah. Winter of eighty-one was a mere bit of a blow, Pulaski. Look at last summer. Hottest and driest ever, all the poison plants surviving while good grass didn't. Water, gone all to alkali. That's a pendulum sign, mind you. Hot summer, cold winter. Other things, too. Beaver piling up sapling cuts like they gone out of style. Cottonwood bark twice the usual thickness. Furry little animals growing fur double thick. And the birds — bunching together like coveys of holy sisters in a flock of sinners."

"But the snow," Aimee said. "Then, we'll be here all winter, Mr. O'Herlihy. Stranded, is it not?"

"Hardly that, ma'am. Directly this storm's over, if it ain't too cold, we'll make it out horseback."

Shallot and Albie had come back in as the driver was talking. Shallot stood listening, his face slightly pinched with cold.

"In any case the blizzard's slacked off for

101

now," he said. "The wind's down — only a few flakes of snow falling. As soon as it's first light, Polack. You, girl. Is that coffee ready?"

From the annex drifted a long, delirious wail. Shallot sat down, crossed his boots, and glanced at Parnell. "Go on, go on. Take a look at him."

Parnell stiffly rose and went into the turkey trot. Presently Anna came out carrying the coffeepot and some cups, and set them on the table. She eyed Raven with a brief venom.

The whole side of her face was darkly swollen, but her catty, long-legged walk was still beautiful to watch. Her full breasts strained at the slack-fitting man's shirt, their round underswells stressed by two cupping shadows. Her hair was brushed out but not bunned again. It hung forward in a thick rope over her right shoulder and was glossy as a horse chestnut.

Watching her, Raven had a firm association of fresh-baked bread in some farm kitchen when he was a kid. A wholesome flavor of remembrance that suggested a host of things a man got to thinking could have been but had never been. An indefinable sadness welled in him. It faded just as promptly.

Aimee said, "I will help you make the breakfast, Anna."

"Is no need you help."

Parnell emerged from the turkey trot. There was a pasty sheen of sweat on his face. "He's in high fever. Calling for a priest."

"Huh," Shallot said. "Did you take his confession?"

"Certainly not. I'm not his padre."

"He won't know the difference, will he? Are you too damned good to ease the last hours of a poor dying Papist of a greaser? Really, Dominie — that's not Christian."

"I think —" Parnell swallowed, his voice paper-dry. "The best thing to do is have another Catholic listen and take his confession to a priest later."

"That so?" Shallot got up and sauntered to the table. He poured a cup of coffee and glanced at Cernak, who was sunk in a surly brooding. "You. Polack."

Cernak did not look up. Shallot jammed his boot against an empty chair and skated it sideways. It rapped Cernak's knee and he jerked erect with a grunt.

"You Polacks are Catholic, aren't you? Take his confession."

"I am Catholic," Aimee said. "If —"

"Stay out of this," Parnell told her harshly.

All eyes turned on him. It was the first halfway spirited reaction he had made yet. Standing before the entrance to the turkey trot, he colored under their stares but kept his eyes on his wife.

"I'll not have you involved in this — this travesty."

A rising anger tinted her face. "It was agreed when we married, James. Your faith for you, my faith for me. I did not think it would work — a minister's wife! But you said it could be. Now —"

"That's not it," Parnell said angrily. He pointed a finger at Shallot. "Don't you see what he's doing? Nothing is sacred to him! He's mocking all religion. Yours, mine, everyone's!"

"Even so, that poor fellow has a right to this comfort, James. It is the way we are taught."

"Argh," growled O'Herlihy. He planted both hands on the table and pushed to his feet. "Look, the O'Herlihys ain't Northern Irish. I'm no great shakes for churchgoing, but I can take his blasted confes—"

"Shut up, Paddy." Shallot smiled in that toothy, mirthless way of his. "Let the lady do as she wishes."

"No." Parnell set his feet apart and fisted his hands. "Before God, she won't."

"Albie," Shallot said softly. "Move that Gospel-clouter out of the way."

Aimee had been looking in astonishment at her husband. Now her alarmed glance flashed to Albie, who was swinging his bulk toward the minister.

"No!" She directed a frantic appeal to Shallot. "It is not worth this. Please, stop him!"

"Sic him, Dominie," Shallot laughed. "A mighty fortress is thy God — eh?"

Again Raven saw that peculiar look on his face. Less of lust than of impersonal curiosity — as if Shallot stood apart from all this and yet was absorbed by its ferment of potential violence, trying to delve its meaning.

Parnell had gone white around the lips. He moved in a sidelong circle away from the chunky outlaw. Albie moved after him with a hoggish smile.

O'Herlihy came around the table, grinning toughly. "Leave the parson alone. I'll take you on, you ugly brute."

Shallot sent him an irritable glance. "Stay out of this, Paddy."

O'Herlihy walked directly over to Albie, who gave him a sullen, wary sizing-up as he growled, "I ain't a-fighting you."

O'Herlihy spat full in his face. "How

d'ye like that, you silly-looking scut?"

Albie pawed at the spittle dripping from his chin. "You dirty son of a bitch!" he bawled, grabbing at the pistol rammed in his belt.

"Albie!"

Shallot's voice crushed Albie's anger to putty. His face sagged. The ruddy stain of rage ran out of it.

Shallot swung to his feet, kicking a chair out of his path as he came forward. His eyes nailed O'Herlihy with the intentness of the same kid, now driving pins slowly through his de-winged fly. O'Herlihy had spoiled his pleasure.

"That was stupid, Paddy. Now you'll fight him. My way." He pulled his gun. "Turn around." His bony chuckle. "Albie. Get that piece of rawhide hanging on the wall. Tie his hands."

O'Herlihy's grin faded. Then he bared his teeth in a wide, strong laugh. He held out his hands, wrists together. Shallot shook his head. "Behind you."

Albie lifted the tangle of rawhide thongs from a wall peg and cut off a length. He bound O'Herlihy's wrists at his back, yanking the knots cruelly tight.

"I'll take your knife, Albie — and your gun," Shallot said. "Square off, gentlemen."

"Irish!" Anna's voice was appalled, faintly horrified. "You no do this. He kill you!"

O'Herlihy spat across the corner of his lip. "Stay clear, Anna mavournin. I'll want scads of room to drop this scut in."

"George," Terrill said. He was leaning on the bar with both hands, so groggy from steady drinking that he could hardly focus his stare.

Shallot flicked him a slack, disinterested look. "Watch this, Quintus. It should prove instructive and amusing."

Raven was aware that Shallot had been watching him from the corner of his eye all the while. This might even be Shallot's way of taunting him to try something. Shallot had his gun out, and Dolph and Cullin would back him no matter what he did.

O'Herlihy shifted away from Albie's lumbering advance in a light, mincing circle, weight on the balls of his feet. He moved like a panther. The floor was broad and clear, giving him plenty of room to maneuver.

Standing a few inches shorter than Albie, he was about two-thirds Albie's weight. Not that Albie was fat, just chunkily muscled. But Raven guessed that in a fair fight, the driver would tear him to pieces. O'Herlihy was as powerful as he was quick, but only speed could help him now.

Albie was following him cautiously, but O'Herlihy shrewdly wore that caution away. He rounded on Albie with a rich Gaelic invective. The kind Raven had heard an occasional Irish teamster spewing at his mules. O'Herlihy was merely being considerate of the ladies, but his meaning couldn't have been clearer in English.

Raging, Albie charged the Irishman. O'Herlihy wheeled out of his path and thrust a foot between Albie's legs. His momentum bulled him past as he crashed to the splintery floor, skidding on his face.

He labored to his feet, the left side of his face scraped raw from chin to temple and bleeding in several places.

Again he drove heedlessly at the Irishman. O'Herlihy retreated a few nimble steps, then hooked his foot around a chair and kicked it in front of Albie. His feet tangled in the rungs and again plunged him solidly to the floor.

He lay dazed and squirming. O'Herlihy could have walked over and kicked him bloody — and Raven guessed he would have done just that had his hands been free. But O'Herlihy was a gamecock of pure pride. He held back, his eyes bright with contempt.

On his feet once more, Albie went after O'Herlihy in a thick, lurching run. Bloody-faced and snarling, he didn't try for the driver with his hands. Instead he crowded O'Herlihy as closely as he could with savage kicks. The Irishman kept dancing out of reach. All of Albie's kicks fell short. He was starting to flounder wearily.

At last by wild clumsy lunges he managed to block O'Herlihy off and finally press him back to a corner. O'Herlihy couldn't evade the next kick. It caught him under the kneecap.

His leg crumpled beneath him. With hands tied, he pitched helplessly forward. And Albie, with a howl of glee, smashed his lifted knee into the Irishman's face as he fell.

Albie began working him over with the boots.

A choking cry escaped Anna. She rushed to the nearest fireplace and snatched up a poker and ran straight at Albie.

He lumbered around, raising a hand to ward off her blow. The other hand made a fist like a knotty ham, ready to smash her down.

Anna swung the poker. Albie's clublike

palms smacked it aside. But his fist never landed. His scream blended with a gunshot.

Raven was on his feet, a thread of smoke trickling from his pistol barrel. It had been no trick to draw his gun unnoticed, with everyone's attention on the fight. He'd known that yelling a warning would not have stopped Albie.

The big outlaw sunk down on his knees, whimpering like a kicked pup. The bullet had smashed through his clenched hand. And a hand pulverized by a .45 at short range was not pleasant to see.

Shallot's eyes were hot, pale kernels in his frost-pinked face. He never quit grinning. "One of us could get you, Milton. One of us."

"Then, you try," Raven said. "And then you're dead."

He cocked the gun. The noise it made was deadly and specific. The fires crackled. No other sound. And nobody moved.

8

The fight seemed to have vicariously gotten something out of Shallot's system. Now that it was over, he seemed bemused and indifferent. Even his skin looked more bloodless than usual. When Albie whined about his hand, Shallot brushed him aside wearily. "Tie a rag around it."

Raven and Parnell carried the unconscious driver into the annex and eased him into a bunk.

"Odd," Parnell whispered. "At the seminary we used to debate academically whether or not the Devil existed. What fools we were to doubt it!"

"Wouldn't go spieling that too loud, I was you," Raven told him.

"Why not? The comparison flatters His Satanic Majesty in there."

"How does the shamrock look to you?"

Parnell stooped down. He raised one of O'Herlihy's eyelids with his thumb and peered into the pupil. He ran both hands along the driver's rib cage. Then he unbuttoned O'Herlihy's shirt and laid his ear to the massive chest. He stood up, shaking his head.

"No broken ribs, at least. But I don't like his look. I think he's badly hurt, but can't really tell till he comes out of it. Of course he was kneed in the face, but I don't think that's to account. Didn't that fellow kick him in the head once?"

"Twice," Raven said.

Anna came in with a pan of steaming water. Impatiently brushing them aside, she knelt beside the bunk and carefully bathed the Irishman's face. His nose was a pulpy wreck.

Mendez had subsided. His yells had become little trickling moans. "Better have another look at him," Raven told the minister.

Parnell uncovered the leg. Raven felt his skin starting to gooseflesh even before the knee was entirely exposed.

"That's got to come off, mister. You know it does."

"I'm not a doctor," Parnell said. He sounded like a mechanical toy with a single refrain.

"I think you mentioned it."

Doctor or not, Raven thought, Parnell had enough medical skill to be justified in operating under the circumstances. But how in hell could you force a scared man to do something like that?

A sound in the doorway. Cernak stood there. He faintly shrugged his great shoulders and said gruffly, "You want, I will take the Mex's confession."

"Up to you," Raven said.

It was a farce. The fever had scrambled Mendez' brains. He gave his confession in a rambling, disjointed mixture of Spanish and English. He called Cernak "Padre." He fancied himself back in the little village church of his boyhood; he made his voice a childish treble. He attributed to other men things that Raven knew Mendez himself had done, and took their sins on his head.

Raven walked wearily back to the common room and poured his first drink from the rotgut keg. He needed it. Shallot left the table and sauntered over.

"I ought to be put out with you, Milton. However. Bygones, eh?"

"You ever get tired of moving people around like pieces on a chess board?"

Interest flared in Shallot's eyes. "You've played chess?"

"Watched it played."

"True in a way, I suppose," Shallot mused. "At least since life has robbed me of every role but the observer's. This damned thing in my chest jades a man's appetites. So I egg on others and study their actions. Like any scientist with a yeasty culture under his microscope, I'm impatient to see what develops."

"You must be hard up."

"As hard up as you?" Shallot idly swirled the liquor in his cup. "What drives you, Milton? I'm really curious. You're an intelligent man, more than able-bodied, still fairly young. You really hate this life. You know Cullin is a hopeless case. Yet you refuse to shake loose. Every man's driven by something. What is it with you?"

Raven shrugged.

"I'll tell you, then. It's the kid. Realistically, you know you can't save him. Huh-uh. What keeps you going is that hope springs eternal. Somewhere in your belly lurks the conviction that someday, somehow, things are going to be better." Shallot's skull-grin flickered and went. "You're Mister Hardcase himself on the front. Underneath, you're another Quintus. Mired in an irrational wallow of dreams and ideals. And other lies of the same genre."

"Maybe. You ought to know."

Shallot chuckled lightly. "You loose a shaft at sarcasm and hit truth between the eyes. Of course. Every cynic is a destroyed idealist. Absolute prerequisite to honest cynicism. Well . . ."

He swallowed the rotgut left in his cup, then glanced at the common room's east window. Like half the windows in the house, it was unglassed. Covered by a square of deerhide scraped fine and rubbed with grease till it was transulcent. Through its thick furring of frost you could see the first glow of dirty light staining the east sky where it veed down between the darkly pale shoulders of Blizzard Pass.

Shallot gave his cup two sharp raps on the bar. "Gentlemen!"

They all looked at him, and he went on: "There are three sets of snowshoes. They'll furnish Cernak and two others." Skullgrin. "One of the two will be me, so that settles half the argument. Now —"

"Guess I'll stay," Cullin said with a sleepy grin.

Raven slid him a grim glance. No need to second-guess Cullin's reason. That meant he was staying too.

He said so.

Shallot nodded. "Dolph?"

The Negro huddled in his blanket near the fire. He gave the frost-whorled window a glance and faintly shuddered. "Got no taste for rousting out in this weather," he growled. "Not 'less I have to. T'other hand, I don't trust you for sour apples, Captain. All that loot — wonder if you could just keep yourself from cutting away over the mountains directly you got hands on it."

Shallot smiled mirthlessly. "Probably not, if I were stupid enough. I'd have to make the attempt alone. On foot. Across the worst mountain country in the West. Through snowdrifts. In subzero weather. And my state of health precarious as it is. Slightly suicidal, wouldn't you agree? Anyhow, you all trust Quintus, and he'll be the one to side me."

"What?" Terrill said.

"Everybody else has passed, old boy. Leaves you. So shove the cork in the bottle and get your coat."

"Wait a minute —" Terrill shook his head as though to clear it. "This is no weather to go tramping up a mountain. The wind has dropped, but it's still snowing some. Suppose the blizzard picks up again?"

"Suppose it does? It's only four miles up, the Polack says. Even if the trail's bad, we

116

should be back by late afternoon."

"It's foolish," Terrill argued. "Be sensible to wait till the weather's cleared."

"Quintus, we can't afford the luxury of a delay. In the first place, when the stage fails to show up in Silverton, you can bank on a few hardy souls strapping on snowshoes and coming to look for it, thinking it might be bogged down in a drift and the passengers need help. Second, if the blizzard does resume and the damned snow gets any deeper, we'll be stuck for the winter. No. What makes sense is, we go now."

"Cap'n George," Albie whispered, "you ain't never left me out of nothing."

"Why, you're part of everything, Albie. But you can't go up a mountain with that hand. Besides" — Shallot flashed a warm and winning grin — "I'll want someone down here seeing after my interests."

Albie straightened up painfully. "Yessir, Cap'n George!"

The little bastard did have a way about him, Raven reflected. It let him exert command over his crew at times when other leaders might lose their men.

They ate breakfast, and Anna put up sandwiches. The snowshoes were brought down from the loft. The three lashed them on and stepped out into the gray, growing dawn. They tramped away between the old buildings and came to the first gradual lift of canyon wall that formed the base of a great squashed peak.

Raven stood outside the station, hands plunged deep in his mackinaw pockets. He watched the forms of the three men grow smaller on the white climbing mantle of the slope. Cernak's heavy form slogged in the lead with a strong plowing stride. The slight form of Shallot labored behind him, and Terrill brought up the rear.

Raven looked at the sky. If its fishgut gray held any portents, he couldn't tell what they might be. He stamped his feet and went back into the station.

"Man," Dolph said glumly, "I'd feel easier it was you going up with 'em 'stead of Quintus."

Raven hung up his mackinaw and stepped over to the fire. He held out his hands to its ruddy aura. "I'd think you'd trust Quintus."

"I trust him. *He's* too trusting, what I don't like. Man could easy tumble off a snowy trail and fall down a ravine."

Raven saw his meaning. But he thought it over and shook his head. "I don't think so. He and Shallot have been friends a long time. Reckon that's about the only senti-ment Shallot has left . . . but it's real enough."

"Yeh," grumbled Dolph. "Far as it goes."

"It's like Shallot said. Sure he might get rid of Cernak and Quintus and take off with the loot. But how far would he get?"

The morning dragged on. So did the waiting. Nobody felt like talking. Anna busied herself in the kitchen or pretended to, and made her son stay close to her.

The two Parnells remained in the annex to do whatever they could for O'Herlihy and Mendez. The latter kept up his weak fluttering cries of pain. But after a while these gradually diminished.

At last Parnell came out of the turkey trot in his shirtsleeves, looking drawn and exhausted. To Raven's question he shook his head. "Both the same. The Mexican's sleeping."

He glanced at Albie, who was hunched in a chair in the corner. A blood-gobbeted rag was knotted around his hand and he was gripping his arm above the wrist to numb the agony. Little squeaking grunts of pain kept escaping him.

Parnell went over to him. "Let me see that."

Albie raised his pain-whipped gaze. "You gonna help me too, Reverend?" He was incredulous.

"Of course," Parnell said tiredly. "Hold out your hand."

After examining Albie's wound, the minister stepped to the kitchen door and said, "Mrs. Kosciusko, could you supply some more hot water?"

"You be such fool to help him?" she demanded.

"I guess so."

"So, well, I be fool too."

When the water was hot, she carried it out to Parnell, giving Raven the usual look of raw, undisguised hatred as she went past him.

He was getting fed up. Her soul-felt horror at their first meeting. The hatred ever since. Even the fact that he had saved her from a second savage bruising by Albie had made no difference.

The hell with it. He might as well have a look at the weather. You couldn't tell much from in here, but the wind seemed to be rising once more.

Shrugging on his coat, he stepped out. The wind slapped silvery whisks of snow against his face. The sky was in turmoil again. Clouds were building above the peaks, driving rapidly out of the north.

The letup had been temporary, as Terrill had guessed. By now he, Shallot, and Cernak must have reached the mineshaft or were close to it. With the storm about to resume full fury, they should have sense enough not to tackle the trail back now. The old shaft would provide refuge till the blizzard had played out.

Raven shivered in the biting wind and turned back to the door. As he pushed it open he heard Cullin's voice — loud, strident, ugly.

"All right, Preacher, goddam you. Drink it!"

Raven stepped in and closed the door. James Parnell was seated at the table; his wife had joined him. Cullin was leaning forward across the table, holding out a cup. The Parnells stared at him, their faces slightly blanched. Cullin set the cup on the table and skidded it across. It sloshed on Parnell's sleeve.

"I said drink, goddam your gospel guts!"

"Cull," Raven said quietly.

His brother's bloodshot stare swung.

"You had it, kid," Raven said. "You want to drink, you're over twenty-one. But you leave these people alone. You toe across the line again, I'll knock you butt over tea-kettle."

Cullin's mouth pursed cruelly as he listened. He said, "Try that, big bro. Try. Maybe we'll see."

"That was a promise, boy. No maybes."

They stood that way for half a minute, and neither man moved a muscle. Raven felt a little sick. They had scrapped before, but he had never seen Cullin's face look like this. He didn't waver, though. He had meant it. The fact was seeping home to Cullin. Abruptly he swung away from the table and went back to the bar.

9

"Thanks," Parnell said, not too shakily. "What's it like out there?" Raven shucked off his mackinaw and tossed it across a chair. He slacked into another chair, facing the Parnells across the table. "Getting worse. You want to hear how to really thank me?"

Parnell shook his head very slightly and lowered his eyes.

"How long you reckon before that leg turns gangrenous?"

Parnell looked up again. "If I amputate," he whispered, "and that boy dies, what does it make me?"

"Either way it goes, it could make you a man. He may die if you do. He'll damned well die if you don't."

Impatience touched Raven. He creaked forward in his chair, scowling at the minister. "I call that a clear choice. I don't get you, Reverend. If there's one man here got an anchor that don't drag, it should be you."

"Anchor —"

"Yeah. Faith." Raven shook his head. "Something I never been able to have and never missed either. But I seen men who had it do things I couldn't. If —"

"Faith!"

Aimee Parnell's laugh slashed through his words like glass splintering. "Oh, forgive me, m'sieur! But faith. That word applied to James Parnell. It is too much!"

"Aimee!"

"Oh, faith he has, Mr. Raven. The kind you mean. He believes in God and in his church and its doctrines. What James lacks is faith in himself — as a man. And that he lost long before he became a preacher. But that faith, I think, should have come first — no, m'sieur?"

"Aimee," Parnell whispered.

"My God, m'sieur, haven't you guessed? Of course he's a doctor! A skilled surgeon. See!" She seized her husband's right hand and held it palm up. "Take off a leg? Pah! You see this hand? In it is the skill to open a man's head — take out a tumor or a bit of depressed bone that would mean death or madness otherwise —"

Her words had spilled out in a vehement

flood. Suddenly she stood up, so quickly that she knocked over her chair. "Oh, excuse me. I cannot help it! He is such a coward, and I am so sick of . . . excuse me."

She turned blindly from the table and half ran into the turkey trot to the annex.

Parnell sat board-stiff. His face was white as paper. "I'm sorry. She's . . . she's never broken out in such a way before. I guess all that's happened —"

"A doctor," Raven said.

"Yes, yes," Parnell said irritably. "Not a practicing one." After a moment he raised one hand — a gesture of weary defeat. "All right. The story. It's not much. I trained in medicine . . . set my hopes on being a surgeon. My first patient died under my knife."

"Your fault?"

"I'd . . . I'd been carousing with some cronies the night before. My hands . . . Anyway I abandoned my surgical career . . . entered the seminary in the hope that a religious vocation would prove my calling."

"What that sounds like," Raven said dourly, "you ran out on the real issue."

"I came to that conclusion — finally. When I did, I commenced to feel guilty about my soft and comfortable Boston pastorate. Oh, not all at once, but the feeling grew. At last my bishop consented to send me to a Western post. Spreading the word in a tough mining camp. A real challenge, I told myself. Aimee . . ."

He slowly massaged his palm over his neck. "Aimee said it was just another way of evading my real shame. God help me. She was right."

Raven reached across and closed a hand over his arm. "You used up all your excuses, then. Ain't you?"

Parnell said in a dead voice, "I can't."

"Maybe not. But you'll try if I got to tie a knife in your hand."

"A knife? My God, I've no instruments —"

"High country miners've made do with butcher knives and hacksaws."

"I need a proper table. Er, restrainers — straps —"

"There's enough men here to hold him."

Parnell's face looked squeezed and desperate. "No narcotic —"

"Whiskey'll do. It'll have to."

From the kitchen came a sudden scuffling noise. Then the boy Laddie's angry cry and a woman's voice lifting in pain. Occupied with outflanking Parnell's objections, Raven had taken the barest notice of

Cullin passing behind his chair to enter the kitchen.

Now he pushed his chair back and reached the kitchen door in two loping strides.

Laddie sprawled on the floor, bleeding from the mouth. Cullin had Anna backed across the sinkboard, his hand knotted in the thick loops of her hair. He was yanking her head back at a brutal angle.

Something flashed in Anna's hand. Cullin gave a yell of startled pain. He caught her wrist and backhanded her savagely. A small knife clattered from her hand to the floor.

All this in the few seconds it took Raven to skirt the table. Anna started to sink to the floor, but Cullin got both hands around her neck. His thumbs tightened.

Raven reached them. He grabbed Cullin by the collar and heaved him around like a sack of meal. "I warned you, boy —"

Cullin's face shocked him. It was twisted into an animal snarl; there was a mad, glaring sheen on his eyes. He tried to swing. Raven batted his arm down, slapped him twice with solid, cuffing blows, and flung him sideways to the floor.

Cullin, his arms flailing, skidded two feet across the floor. His head met the stone fireplace with a wicked thunk.

Raven felt sick and shaken as he could not remember feeling in his whole life. So that was how Cull had looked to that girl — the first one. It had not happened according to the self-extenuating version Cullin had given him. It couldn't have.

Raven turned, bent, and lifted the little boy to his feet. He wasn't hurt except for a cut lip. He gave Raven a fearless, wide-eyed regard, then went to his mother. Anna dropped to her knees and held him tightly.

"You all right?" Raven asked.

"Is no thanks that brother yours." She rubbed her throat, her voice rasping and choked. "He is crazy! Why you no have him lock up?"

"You wasn't swinging your hips all over the place," Raven growled, "it wouldn't of happened."

Cullin was out cold. Raven stooped, grabbed him by the wrists and hauled him up, and ducked to let Cullin collapse across his shoulder. He tramped out of the kitchen as Anna — for a moment speechless with surprise and rage — spluttered loose a tirade of foreign words.

Raven carried his brother into the annex and dumped him into a bunk. Aimee

Parnell looked on in surprise. She was sitting by O'Herlihy's bunk, laying warm compresses on his forehead.

Besides the nasty rap on his scalp, Cullin's sleeve was ripped from elbow to wrist, showing a long, shallow cut. Her slash had hardly broken the skin, but it beat all hell where she had gotten the knife.

Raven glanced over toward Mendez, who was awake, seemingly rational, and faintly grinning. He raised a hand weakly, beckoning Raven to his side.

"How you doing, Billy?"

"You know something, amigo? I think she be all right, the leg." Mendez' eyes were bright as a bird's. His grin kept coming and going. "I feel this in my bones. Soon she be all right. You take the look at her, eh?"

Raven said, "Sure," and began removing the soiled bandage. He had looked at the leg a little earlier. Even so, he couldn't hide all his reaction.

Mendez, watching his face, whispered, "What is it, amigo?"

"Better see for yourself."

"I can't lift up so high, Milton. You got to help me."

Raven slid an arm under Billy's shoulders and raised him nearly to a sitting position. Mendez gasped and winced with the pain of this small movement. He peered at the knee.

"Jésus Maria. Amigo —" He clutched at Raven's arm like a child grabbing for reassurance.

"That's got to come off, Billy."

"What?" Mendez' eyes, yellow-tinged at the corners, rolled toward him. He thrust savagely with both hands, shoving Raven away. He fell back with an odd half screech. His eyes went unfocused in the reflex of stabbing pain.

He said in Spanish, "You will not take my leg, hombre."

"You saw it," Raven said stonily.

"Good God, amigo. What is a man without two good legs? He is nothing! How does he ride like the wind? How does he take the eye of a pretty girl? How will he do the things a man must? No, amigo mio! As you are my friend, do not do this to me!"

"A leg don't make a whole man. Keep it on, you lose everything."

"Yes, amigo? Then if it gets so bad, you take the gun —"

"Go to hell, Billy."

Raven tramped out through the turkey

130

trot. He heard Aimee's quick steps behind him. Parnell came slowly to his feet as they reached the common room. Raven's eyes were hard as iron. He looked at Parnell and didn't speak.

Parnell moistened his lips. "All right. You'll help me. Will they?" He nodded at Dolph, then Albie.

"I ain't no goddam servant of yours, white man," Dolph said.

"Mendez ain't white," Raven observed.

"Screw him too. He ain't no brother of mine."

"I guess that's one piece of luck he had."

"You a goddam fool, man. Fewer the better. You cutting down your own share."

"Yours too," Raven said quietly. "You're a prize in any color, Dolph." He glanced at Albie.

For answer Albie raised his good hand. "This one ain't bunged up."

Raven nodded toward the small arsenal of arms and knives stacked in the corner. "Look over the cutlery, Reverend. What'll you need?"

"He will not need that —" Aimee gave a small, shaky laugh. Her eyes glowed. "I brought your case of instruments, James. It is in the bottom of my trunk."

"But I gave those to Bishop Laemmle

before we left — and told him to turn them over to the medical college —"

"Your bishop returned them to me. He is a very wise man. And I brought other things — opiates — everything you will need."

A kind of pale determination touched Parnell's face. "All right. Ask Mrs. Kosciusko to heat some more water." He glanced toward the long trestle table. "That will have to suffice."

The men went back through the turkey trot. Whipflicks of icy wind flowed through chinks in the walls. The flimsy structure shuddered. The blizzard was rising fast; if it kept up like this, it would make last night's blow seem like a May zephyr.

Raven, coming first into the annex, saw that Mendez had hauled himself partly upright in his bunk. He was braced on his elbows. His brown skin glistened in the gray light. His eyes were like a condemned man's.

Parnell went to his wife's trunk, still in the corner where he and O'Herlihy had lugged it last night. He snapped off a catch, raised the lid and rummaged to the bottom. He brought up a large mahogany chest.

"All right, men. Now you can bring him —"

"You don't bring nobody no place,

Padre," Mendez put in very softly.

All had been looking at the chest in Parnell's hands — and now all looked toward Mendez. Raven realized they'd been careless. Billy had his .45 in his hand. Now he cocked it, his lip quivering with the effort. His smile was waxy.

"You don' put the knife to my leg, gringos."

"You figure you can take all of us, Billy?"

"No, Milton. I just get the first one that sticks his head back in here. I blow his goddam head clean off. *Comprende?* Then nobody else tries. Now" — he waved the gun — "you all get out."

Suddenly Dolph stepped from the turkey trot, his gun in hand. "Figured you might need a friend, Billy."

Mendez swung the .45 toward him. "Don't you go give me that!" His voice was shrill with suspicion. "You got no friends, Dolph!"

"You wrong, man. I'm gonna show you how wrong."

Dolph rammed his gun in the holster and came across the room, his bony, long-fingered hands held out from his body, palms up.

"Look here, Billy. What you say t'this . . ."

Dolph simply walked up to the bunk and

slapped a palm down over Mendez' .45, so easily and casually that his movements blended like a long friendly gesture.

Mendez jerked the trigger.

Dolph grimaced. He made a fist around the cylinder and trigger guard and then yanked the gun from the Mexican's weak hold.

Dolph let up the hammer, and Raven saw the blood dripping off his right thumb. Dolph, in the instant of grabbing the gun, had jammed his thumb between hammer and breech. The firing pin had gouged deep into the flesh.

"Only way I could, him on cock," Dolph said.

"Dolph!" Mendez screamed. "You black bastard! I kill you for this! You hear me? I kill you!"

"Can't hear you a-tall, man." Dolph tugged out a bandanna and wadded it around his thumb. "Like I said. Figured you might need a friend."

Raven wasn't too surprised. An embittered man generally had values to start with. Then it wasn't his values he shed so much as his hopes, his dreams. He understood Dolph. As well as a white man could. He didn't suppose that was any too well.

"I kill you all," Mendez wept. "I string

your goddam *cojones* from my belt. *Bastardos! Chingados!* Oh, for the love of the good God, amigos, don't do this."

Parnell told them how to hoist Mendez gently from the bunk and carry him out to the table. They shuffled awkwardly into the dog trot, four men supporting the sobbing, feebly struggling Mexican between them.

Behind them Cullin let out a soft groan. He was coming to.

Parnell said hesitantly, "Hadn't I better look at your brother?"

"He'll keep," Raven said.

10

As she lifted her coat off a peg Anna heard Billy Mendez crying and cursing while the men carried him into the common room, Parnell telling them in his cultured, nervous tones to put the Mexican on the table, and Raven warning them to do it easy. Raven's voice struck a strange chord on her ear. Probably because she had only heard it before while she was watching him and hadn't paid it much attention. It was deep, even, reassuring. Not ugly like his face. And it made clear that he, not Parnell, was in real charge of this situation.

Then she caught herself, remembering. What was she thinking? That ugly face of his! Her hand clenched with bruising force around the jacket folds.

Aimee was bent down by the fireplace, testing with her finger a pan of water heating on the embers. Now she stood and straightened around. Her eyes widened.

"Anna — but you are not going out in such weather!"

Anna pointed at the nearly empty wood-box. "Now is time to get in my wood. Before storm get worse. I go quick. Ladislas!"

Laddie sat at the small kitchen table, scraping clean a preserves jar with an iron spoon and worrying the spoon clean with his tongue. "*Da,* Mama?"

The English word pleased her. He was starting to learn. Anton had bawled her out for not learning English faster. ("You got an example to set the boy, sister. God's whiskers, you want him to grow up talking like a dumb Polack?")

Anton was right. Yet he had been in this country for twenty-three years, not just six months, and a Polish flavor was still thick in his speech. It was hard to learn a new language when all these months there was no one to talk to but poor Gabe, Anton with his monosyllabic grunts (you might as well learn English from a shoat), and Irish, whom she rarely saw and who then wanted only to poke fun or make love.

She stooped and held out her arms. Laddie slipped from the chair and ran to her. She held him gently at arm's length. "Ladislas. No Russian. Say, 'Yes, Mama.'"

"Yes, Mama," he said promptly.

She smiled and shook her head. So like Stephen! Quick and smart. And stubborn. He knew the words well enough but rarely said them except on order. Stephen's son, even to the slight fearless tilt of head.

"Little Mother, do you cry?"

"Only a tear or two. Must I ask your leave to shed them, my big son?"

"I don't like to see you cry," he said seriously.

She smiled and ruffled his hair. "You will look after the pretty lady. I go for wood."

She stood up and slipped on her coat. It was really a hunting shirt. Irish had killed the three deer needed to make it, had shown her how to cure and work the soft, aromatic buckskin. It was loose-sleeved with a shoulder cape and a hood you secured with a drawstring. So voluminous that it reached to her knees, it lapped deeply over in front so that a belt let you use the folds as pockets.

Anna unlatched and swung open the door. She stepped quickly out and pulled it tight against the wind's driving fury. She half skirted the building on its lee side, then made a dash for the woodshed.

She was no weakling, but the two hundred feet of wintry maelstrom between house and woodshed nearly drove her off her feet. The ominous, churning sky of minutes ago was blotted out now by sheeting snow.

She raised the swing bar that secured the woodshed door, then had to fight the wind with all her weight in order to drag the door open.

Suddenly a gloved hand smacked against its edge just above her mitten and pulled, aiding her. Anna whirled around. Her gasp was torn voicelessly away on the wind. She came close to panic in that instant — seeing whose face it was inches from hers.

"Get inside!" Raven yelled above the shrill yammer of wind.

When she didn't stir, he pushed her through the door and followed, pulling it shut behind them.

Anna took two backward steps, flattening her spine against the nearest wall. "What you want?"

Raven eyed her with the thinnest sort of patience. "Preacher's wife said you went out for wood. I aimed to see that was all."

"What you — oh!" Her laugh crackled in the cold air. It brimmed with so much relief that she felt obliged to give the last note or two a mocking tinge. "Maybe you afraid I got gun out here. Is so?"

"Maybe. You're pretty handy on pulling

a knife out of nowhere."

"So?" The reference made her think of something else. Her face flamed. "Listen, you! I no swing my hips."

Raven ignored her. He circled the dim interior and studied each wall, the few shelves and niches, finally the pile of sawed cedar lengths that filled nearly half the shed. He halted by the chopping block and pulled out the ax sunk in it. He idly tested the edge with the ball of his thumb while he scanned the walls.

"Boo!" Anna said.

He gave her an unconcerned glance. She laughed at him, her eyes taunting and mocking. Which was foolish, she knew, but she couldn't help herself. How she hated him!

Raven moved across to the big grindstone. "Turn it," he told her, still looking around him.

Anna hesitated, then came over and seized the crank. She made the huge, circular stone whine. Raven gave all his attention to the ax bit then, holding the edge to a perfect bevel.

She eyed his bent head close up. *Raven.* The name didn't fit him every way. A raven was black; he was very fair. But looking at the fiercely gaunt face helped her picture a bird of prey that ate the eyes from dead animals. Ugh! Buzzard would be better (evil eyes, cruel-beaked nose), but Raven would do.

Strange. He was standing very close and they were completely alone, yet she didn't fear him anymore.

All right! Maybe it was unreasonable to hate a man for wearing a face like that Russian officer's. He was certainly a better man than the others. But he'd come here with them, hadn't he? He was after the same stolen money . . . or was he?

His brother? Well, she'd thought before that that *might* be it. But all of it? She wasn't sure.

He thumb-tested the bit again. She could see that the edge was very keen. She had to taunt him again: "Maybe now you be afraid to give me ax."

"No reason to be," Raven said dryly. "This was a favor for a favor."

"What favor?" Anna said suspiciously.

"Same one. You been sharpening an ax for me since we met, ain't you? Here."

He held out the ax, and she took it. He walked to the door and paused there, his prey-bird's eyes unreadable. "Hurry up with that wood." He went out before she could answer, banging the door shut after him.

She glared her hate at the door. At least he might have offered to split the wood for her. Of course she would have refused, but he might have offered.

Angrily unsure of her feelings — hating the fact — she set a chunk of cedar on the block and split it with a clean whack. But her indignation was soon blunted in the quick, steady rhythm of the chopping — hard work even for a strong woman.

She did not like the increasing wail of the storm. It was unnerving. So was the trembling batter of its fists on the old shed.

Six months at the far end of nowhere had palled her spirit. She had been accustomed all her life to the cosmopolitan color and sound of Warsaw. Here: glaring skies, vaulting peaks, limitless distance. Crudest of living conditions and the eternal howl of wind in the pass. The sole fleck of excitement provided by the rare arrival of the stage (true until last night anyway).

The worst part of all was the loneliness. But she could stand that too. She and Laddie were young and strong and well — was that not something? When the time came (and she would make it soon) they would leave this place and she would hire out for her keep at a farm or ranch on one side of the mountains or the other. She didn't care, as long as they were near a town and a good school. Her boy would grow up to do her proud . . .

Bemused, working with a hard, steady swing, she lost track of time.

She gave a start when the shed door grated on the frozen earth, then swung outward. A flurry of wind and snow whipped through the shed. The dark figure of a man stepped through. He grabbed the door and pulled it shut with a powerful heave.

Anna gripped both hands around the ax haft as Cullin turned, grinning, to face her. She tasted a black bile of fear in her throat as she backed off from the chopping block.

Cullin followed her step by step. He was in no hurry, and he was chuckling quietly.

Anna's heel touched the wall. She could not back any farther, so she edged along the wall to one corner. And she had to stop.

She knew that screaming would do no good. The wind would drown her out. She was completely alone with this crazy boy. And he was keeping carefully between her and the door.

She had never seen such eyes. A maniac's eyes. Glistening like viscid puddles in the half gloom.

"Go 'way, boy," she said hoarsely. "I kill you."

"Yeah," he whispered. "Fight. That's it. Fight me hard, you big bitch. Yeah. Yeah. Make it good."

This one is all crazy, she thought. *Where is his brother now?* Oh God.

Cullin moved in a hard, quick lunge, in and out, a feint to make her swing the ax. She did. The bright edge grazed his coat, razoring the thick fabric apart where it touched.

She got in only the one swing. In that moment her guard was broken. Cat-quick, Cullin slipped inside it. He cuffed her across the jaw, at the same time twisted the ax from her grasp. Flung aside, it clattered against the wall.

Anna gasped with the pure shock of his palm slamming her swollen jaw. Tears jetted into her eyes. His face was a swimming blur; she went for it with curved fingers.

Cullin grabbed her left wrist. But missed her right one. Her down-slashing nails missed his eye by an inch. They furrowed four red tracks from his left cheekbone to the edge of his jaw.

Cullin smashed her on the chin. Not with his open hand but his fist. Anna fell to the clay floor and rolled on her side. Stunned. Her teeth had split her lip: she could taste the salt of her blood, a raw brassy taste that shocked her half-conscious.

She felt his hands touch her. He was chuckling to himself, mumbling something about "big brother." Saying that he knew where he could take her and big brother would never find them, by Christ.

Then he was lifting her from the floor. Anna was hazily aware of that much. Before a dizzy suffocation of wool-gray darkness overwhelmed her senses, blotting out everything.

All the candles of the gilt chandelier had been lighted, dropping a tawdry yellow pool of light on the trestle table, which had been pulled directly beneath the fixture.

Mendez had been lashed down to the table, turns of rope circling his neck, chest, arms, wrists, and good leg. He was deep in opiates, his injured leg exposed. It was swollen to twice normal size. The knee was a scarlet pulp from which bone oozed like ivory splinters.

The smaller table from the kitchen had been lugged out; Parnell's instruments were laid on it in glittering array. Dolph stood at the head of the table, ready to hammerlock Billy's neck and shoulders at the surgeon's order. Albie stood by the good leg, Raven by the smashed one.

Parnell had given his wife a few instructions. She knew what would be expected of her. She was close to his side and she was very pale. But she looked as ready as the men.

Parnell rammed a roll of linen against Mendez' groin. "Major blood vessels. This'll help control bleeding. Now. Tourniquet."

Aimee handed him a broad leather belt. Parnell fastened it above the linen wad and made it as tight as he could.

"All right, men. Aimee, scalpel —"

The three men clamped down holds on Mendez, reinforcing the grip of the ropes. Momentarily Parnell gazed at the bright blade in his fingers — almost with a fascinated dread. Then he made the first cut.

He cut in a rough pattern at the lower thigh, making the incision as he had explained he would, with two long flaps of muscle that would form a pad between skin and the bone stump.

Even though he was submerged in a dense narcosis, Mendez' shrill screams outdid all his previous efforts.

Raven watched in fascination as the

muscles cleanly parted under the keen steel. Blood from severed vessels bubbled in the fleshy gorge. As fast as it welled, Aimee soaked it up with fresh linen; she clamped on forceps and linen pads as Parnell had shown her, at the places he now indicated. The aplomb of this slender, delicate girl would put a lot of men to shame.

Parnell looped whipcord sutures above the forceps, reducing the blood flow further. He began to cut again. His face gleamed palely; his mouth worked. But his hand was stone-steady. The muscle fibers fell neatly apart under the blade as he worked up from the initial incision.

Mendez was almost quiet now except for an occasional spastic shudder of the ruined leg.

Parnell delicately reversed the scalpel in his hand, using its handle to raise a thick vessel. "Femoral artery," he murmured. He pointed with his left hand. "Clamps, Aimee. Here, and here . . ."

He cut the artery with one stroke and sutured. Next the blue vein was severed by the same process.

"Raise the leg, Mr. Raven."

Parnell made another cut at the back of the elevated leg; the last major bleeders were clamped and sutured. All the fleshy tissue and blood vessels were now severed, and secured against hemorrhaging. Only the thigh bone remained to be cut. That and one thing more — a very slender adjacent column, white and gleaming, that he had avoided.

"I want you men to watch this," Parnell said quietly. He gave the slim column the merest touch of his scalpel. The leg muscles jerked crazily. "You see? That contains the nerves. I want you to brace like hell when I say the word. Worst'll be over then."

Raven was suddenly aware of the steady, remorseless ache in his arms, the drenching crawl of sweat under his clothes. Worse? Could it be any worse? He'd never known the grip of a tension like this. The contempt he had felt for Parnell had evaporated.

Something might have snapped Parnell's courage long ago. But you couldn't doubt that he'd once had it. Because, as far as Raven was concerned, it took guts of boiler steel even to contemplate doing something like this.

Parnell thrust his finger under the nerve and set his knife. "Now —" A deft stroke.

Mendez' whole body arched up in a ter-

148

rible spasm, his trunk and limbs straining against their hands. His scream drowned the rising wail of the blizzard.

Suddenly the screaming ended. His body went limp and flaccid.

"Fainted," muttered Parnell. "Good. Cut femur now and finish up fast. Bone saw."

Aimee handed him the saw. He laid the tempered steel against the thigh bone and began to saw carefully, pushing the muscles up as he worked in order to cut in above the level of incision. The teeth bounced like a jittery seesaw at first, then grooved neatly. Bone dust trickled down.

"Doc," Dolph said huskily. "You better — I think —"

"Not now, man, for God's sake!"

The whine of steel against bone deepened as it met the marrow. In a few seconds the leg came free. It slipped sideways, wet and slick in Raven's hands. He gingerly set it down on the blood-soaked table as Dolph said, "Doc. Goddammit, you look now!"

Parnell moved to the head of the table. A soft hissing sound escaped him. Raven saw now that Mendez lay with his head back, mouth gaping. His eyes were lidded to glazed slits. He was utterly still.

"Get back," Parnell said. "All of you!"

For a frantic half minute he worked over Mendez. Then he turned away from the table. His face was like gray putty.

He said tonelessly, "I won't have to suture the flaps." His voice dropped to an agonized whisper. "Cutting the nerve was too much. Too much for his heart. Oh, Christ. Christ."

It might have been a prayer, but it was more like the moving of a puppet's jaws, woodenly mouthing a puppeteer's rote. No heart. No body. No meaning.

Raven had an uneasy feeling. That he had just watched two men, not one, die in this room.

11

Cernak knew that they had nearly reached the Corona claim, but it was hard going. The snow was banked heavily on the narrow switchback trail, heaping up at a steep angle halfway to a man's thighs on the inner trailside against the rising mountain flank. This forced the three men to negotiate the rim edge, which the wind had broomed almost clean. The rimrock wasn't iced, but its bare surface was perilously slick. The danger was increased by a rising wind, terrific at this height and on the open slope. They had to sway their bodies against its thrust, constantly adjusting to its differing velocities. The three were awkward on their snowshoes, which were of little use under these conditions. In fact they were a handicap when you were fighting the wind. Throw your weight wrong, and you could throw yourself over the rim.

"George!" Terrill yelled. "For God's

sake, let's take cover till this thing blows out! There must be a cave — some sort of cover Cernak knows of —"

"Shut up!" Shallot snapped the words like icicles. "Polack! How much farther?"

"Little ways."

Shallot's impatience was pushing them all hard, Cernak thought. That was good. A pushy man was, finally, a careless man.

So far they had been careful enough with him. They had made him take the lead and break trail. Both men kept their guns out and made sure he never got close. Wise of them. Let him get his hands on either one and he could hardly keep from cracking his neck on the spot. Which would be a pure folly. Especially with his best chance to turn the tables on them just up ahead.

All the same he wished that one of them, preferably Shallot, would make a misstep and go off the rim. He had no doubt of his ability to take one when the moment came. But even with surprise on his side, the other was likely to get him.

He thought of Anna and Laddie. No doubt the girl had meant all she said. But time and a good argument or two might change her mind. Make her see what that money could mean for them.

The thought heated his resolve. Even if

Shallot kept his promise and left them un-harmed (and Cernak was far from sure that he would), he couldn't let him have the money. Not with the future and happiness of his grandchild at stake.

Fortunately they had covered a good three-quarters of the distance to the Corona before the storm had picked up again. Now they were only yards from their destination. A good thing, Cernak thought. The wind was roughening fast, skirling great gusts of snowdust against their leaning bodies.

At the rate it was worsening, he doubted he'd get back to Thirty Mile today. The probability gave him no concern. There was food, matches, in the haversack slung across his shoulder. He could find food and shelter if necessary. Now you get ahead of yourself, he thought humorlessly.

Shallot's almost steady cursing held a dreary monotony. "Why in hell did you cache the loot way up here?"

"Because it's hard to get to." Cernak threw the words back over his shoulder. "You don't find it so?"

Shallot cursed him instead of the weather.

Cernak led them around a naked black shoulder of snow-veined rock; he halted. "There" — he waved a mittened paw.

The deserted works of the Corona Mining Company sprawled like rickety scars across the broad curve of the mountain that had opened up suddenly before them. Furrows of gravel and ore tailings stretched like straggling fingers down the slope. Beyond the first tailing rose the top section of the main-shaft scaffolding. Where the ore tailings thinned away farther down was the old crushing mill and five giant leaching vats supported by a rotting log frame. Nothing remained of the company buildings but tangles of collapsed studding long since stripped of tarpaper and puncheon siding.

Cernak pointed. He swung his thick arm upward at an angle toward a dark spot high on the escarpment. "See? There's the original mineshaft, eh? There I hide the money."

Terrill groaned. "Jesus. It's a good quarter mile up. Do we climb that?"

"We climb." Shallot shut his jaws with a snap. "It had better be there, Polack — that's all. Go ahead."

The crooked trail petered out as the three men tramped into the heart of the old Corona works, up past the crushing mill and the cyanide vats and the main-shaft scaffolding. As they ascended toward the old shaft the footing got more treacherous. A steady wind had drifted the snow into deep pockets and mantled it evenly over the rough spires of rock, on which their snowshoes kept snagging.

At last the three stood in the mouth of the shaft. It cut back into the peakside like a black, gaping maw. They huddled slightly inside, out of the wind, as they removed their snowshoes. Cernak dug out the bull's-eye lantern from his pack and got it lighted.

As he started down the shaft, the lantern high in his fist, Shallot hissed into his ear, "No tricks, Polack. One wrong move. Just one."

Weird moving inkblots of shadow were thrown by their bodies and the large fragments of stone littering the tunnel. Cernak's steps held a groping care; an uneasiness filled his gut.

He hated this place — its dank, dead air, its hollow, clanking echoes, the rotted stulls and crossbeams that had fallen away in some places and in others sagged with ancient strains. Here and there even the slight jarring of their steps was enough to bring earth sifting down.

Just because it was a frightening place to go prowling in, he had hidden the money here. But not very far in. Maybe only a dozen yards, just past the tunnel's first sharp turn.

"Here."

Cernak halted close to one wall and knelt, setting the lantern down. He rolled aside a sizable chunk of rock, then jerked off his mittens and began digging in the rubble with his fingers.

As he worked, Cernak shot an occasional glance at the faces of the two men. They stood no more than nine feet from him and were totally intent on the shallow excavation he was making.

The gravel was quite loose. Anton scooped it out in quick double handfuls. It should be loose. He had last dug up and replaced the money box only two weeks ago. That was a regular precaution of his.

Not that he had been too worried about anyone's finding the money. It was just that when you hid a gun in a box of buried bank loot, it was wise to stay sure that the gun was in working order.

Cernak's nails lightly scraped the surface of the box. He quickly cleared away the dirt covering it. He knew that the others could not see far into the shadowy hole. As he continued to pitch out handfuls of dirt, he gently loosened the sliding lid he had

156

devised for the specially constructed box.

In a few seconds he had completely exposed a heavy Colt that rested on top of the oilcloth wrapping that contained the bank notes. Then he gently closed his fist around the butt.

Shallot leaned forward. "What in hell, Polack? Why'd you stop?"

"Here's why, Captain."

Cernak said it very softly and casually, lifting both hands from the hole as though he were bringing up the box. He eared back the Colt's hammer as he whipped it up. And shot at once.

Too quickly. The bullet screamed off the rock wall not over a foot from Shallot's arm. In the same instant Cernak fired, his arm lashed out. A cuff of his meaty palm flung the lantern against the wall. The tunnel went black in the sudden washout of light.

Cernak flung himself to one side, full-length across the floor. Stabs of gun flame burst the darkness. Both Shallot and Terrill had returned fire, and both shot too high.

Cernak saw the square, bulky shape of Terrill's head and torso against the dim flare of daylight that reached from the tunnel mouth. He fired and heard Terrill's agonized grunt and saw his heavy silhouette drop.

Shallot yelled something as he ran forward, shooting blindly into the darkness. He tripped over Cernak's foot and went sprawling. Cernak twisted on his side and slashed out savagely with his pistol in the half dark and only clanked a rock. He heard Shallot roll away and scramble to his feet.

Cernak fired from the ground. He heard two shrieking ricochets deep in the tunnel. Every shot and its rebounds had picked up a fringe of echoes; the rocky cleft pulsed with a continual pounding roar.

Now Cernak lay very still, straining his ears as the last shot echoes died. He caught the small sounds Shallot made, scuttling away like a crab farther into the tunnel.

There were other noises too. Falling rattle of pebbles and hunks of earth shuddered loose from the ceiling, and Terrill was making heavy, gusting moans of pain and calling wearily, "George! George!"

Cernak felt his way across the littered floor till he touched Terrill's coat. He felt the chest, which was drenched with blood.

"Is . . . that you . . . George?"

Cernak felt down Terrill's arm to his

hand and found Terrill's gun. He rammed it in his own pocket and cocked his Colt.

"Cernak?"

Cernak tucked the pistol muzzle under Terrill's chin. "Go on," Terrill husked. "You've killed me already. It'll be a favor."

"I think so," Cernak grunted. "Then, I don't do it."

He let the Colt carefully off cock and stood up and tramped back to the hole he had dug. He lifted the money-packed oil-cloth free of the box and stuffed it inside his coat as he stepped over Terrill and loped swiftly to the tunnel mouth.

He paused just long enough to strap on his snowshoes and sling the other two pairs across his shoulder. Then he went away down the escarpment in great, plunging strides.

A grin curled his broad mouth. The first such grin in many days. Or was it months?

He had the money. He was armed now. Shallot would never overtake him. And once he reached the station, he would take the remaining gangmen by surprise.

The grin faded. The blood began to boil in his brain. After all his planning and trouble, these bastards had to find him and spoil it. Shallot had destroyed whatever illusions Anna might still have about her father. They had put him on the run again, and maybe he could not persuade Anna to come with him.

Momentarily Anton's regret cut deepest at his failure to kill Shallot. *God damn!* If he'd had to hit only one, Shallot or Terrill, why not Shallot?

His fists flexed and unflexed with each swinging stride he took. There was cold murder in his mind. *I will kill the rest anyway. I will kill all those pigs.*

He achieved the angling shoulder of rock that now blocked the camp from his view and put him back on the narrow trail to Thirty Mile. Here Cernak paused again. One by one he flung the four snowshoes over the rim, watching them arc against the wind and then sail into the pale darkness below.

That would take care of Shallot. Maybe it would even be the death of him. The snow was piling deeper, the wind worsening. That would keep him where he was. And after the storm the cold would set in. Bitter iron-cold that would freeze the frail consumptive's thin blood in his thin veins.

Cernak's lips stirred faintly. It might have been another grin. Then he moved on down the trail in great, strong strides.

After a time he slowed. He was uneasily

studying the sky and the ragged, thickening flurries of snow. It laced against a man's bare face like hand-flung buckshot. The wind tore through his heavy windbreaker as if it did not exist.

He was still more than three miles from Thirty Mile. The blizzard was whipping to a deeper fury by the moment. He could see hardly an arm's length beyond his face. His flesh felt bruised and numb under the continuous slash of snow and wind — a warning in itself. He must get out of this and quickly.

Anton fought another dozen strides along the trail. At a point just ahead was a narrow gorge that split back into the peak a short way. Once, out of mild curiosity, he had followed the small crevasse to its end. It would do to shelter him for as long as the blizzard lasted.

He quickly located the slender opening in the rock and swung into it. At once the wind's force was cut. The walls narrowed down after a few yards. The two rims of the canyon arched almost to a joining above his head. The thin space between them was bridged by a crust of frozen snow.

Anton settled down on his haunches and burrowed his back into the snow, drawing his legs up against his chest. He blinked the watery sting out of his eyes and rubbed his chilled flesh. The bear, they called him. Eh. He would be a goddam bear till the storm was done.

Then, one way or another, he would set to the matter of getting the rest of those bastards who had taken over his station, looked with lust at his daughter, held his grandson for the burning . . .

12

Anna wasn't wholly conscious. But she did feel a succession of dim sensations. First of all, she was being carried. Slung like a bag of flour across a man's broad shoulders. Feeling his slogging strides as he fought his way into the driving teeth of the storm, lurching beneath her weight. Once she heard him curse as he stumbled and then caught his balance. And she felt the pummeling lash of cold and wind through her clothes. She was aware of these things quite weakly and impersonally. She strove to move her arms and legs, to struggle, and she couldn't. All she could manage was a soft cry that whipped away on the wind.

Then they reached the lee of a building. She saw the dark, weathered wall heave like a tossing sea through the whirling whiteness and she knew that Cullin was hugging the wall and working his way toward the front of the building. Next he was tramping onto a wide, sagging veranda.

Anna's senses were sluggishly flooding back. Now she came to just enough to vomit. Cullin cursed and tried to shift her body, but too late to keep most of it from spewing over his shoulder. Still swearing, he dumped her on the porch and turned his attention to the boards nailed across the door. He ripped them off one by one, got the door open, bent and scooped her up again, and carried her inside.

Her wakening senses fed more muddy impressions to her brain. She realized where they were. In one of the few buildings of Thirty Mile that was still fairly intact. She'd had a time last summer trying to keep Laddie from exploring the tumble-down structures, so she was a little familiar with them. This was the old assayer's office.

She began to kick her legs weakly and beat her fists against his head. Cullin dropped her once more, this time to a rough floor. It jarred painfully against her back, and she felt a gouging pain against her shoulder blade.

Cullin knelt beside her. He stripped off his gloves, then reached for the belt of her coat. When she tried to fight him, he cuffed her again. He got her coat open, then began tearing with frenzied fingers at the buttons of her shirt.

Suddenly a blast of icy air swept the room. He had failed to set the latch securely; the door had blown open.

Swearing viciously, Cullin lunged to his feet and went to close it. The wind was still on the rise; now its pressure was so fierce that he had to plant his feet and strain his weight to force the door slowly shut.

The chill inrush of the storm had hit Anna like a shock, reviving her completely. She had a focused, sudden awareness of the object hurting her shoulder blade. She rolled sideways now and groped for it.

A rough-edged piece of streaky ore. One of many such samples that the assayer had kept on his desk. Now they littered the floor all around it.

Anna saw that Cullin had finally got the door closed and was trying to hook the latch firmly in place. The split-log door was so badly warped that his effort to close it tight threatened to crack the ancient hinges.

Anna scanned the floor, searching for the largest chunk of ore. It was about two yards away. She was so weak and dizzy that she could barely flounder over to it on her hands and knees.

Closing her mittened hand over the hefty chunk sent a current of desperate strength through her. She managed to get up on her knees and sway to her feet. Her ears roared with a hundred echoes of the storm; she had to swallow back the hot retching that boiled into her throat.

She looked at Cullin's broad back. Forced herself to take a tottering step. Another. Cullin had the latch fixed in place now. He shook it several times; it held. With a growl of satisfaction, he wheeled around. Anna was less than a yard from him, her fist just bringing the weighty hunk of ore up and back.

Cullin gave a startled grunt. He threw his arm out. She whipped the piece of rock down in a stiff-armed clout. It could have missed easily as not, but in his surprise Cullin was as awkward as she. He failed to block her swing.

The jagged sample took him squarely above the left eye. Cullin howled and grabbed blindly. He caught her arm. But it was the wrong arm, and Anna's other hand swung again, this time at a clear and free target.

The blow was backed by a flood of returning strength — and a cold terror, too. She hit him full in the temple.

Cullin's hand fell from her arm. He staggered back against the door, bowed over with pain. Blood spurted from his gashed scalp. His hands began lifting to his contorted face.

Anna took a step forward. She arced the sample against his head a third time, with as much fury now as fear. His dim moan was choked off. He slid to the floor and sagged sideways on his face.

Anna bent over him, the rock half lifted. She peered at him in the faded light. His head was tilted so that the dark strands of blood ran into his pale hair. Had she killed him? She hoped so. He looked dead.

She knelt down and strained to turn his body enough for her to undo his coat and remove his pistol belt. Her fingers, she was dismayed to realize, were so numbed by cold that she could hardly manage buttons or buckle. Finally she got the belt off and cinched it around her waist and belted her hunting shirt over it.

Now was the time, before the other two returned with her father, to turn tables on the men in the station. She mustn't fail. If she did, she could expect no mercy. Not even from Raven. She had just smashed down his brother.

Anna bent down again, grabbed Cullin

under the arms, and dragged him a laborious couple of feet from the door. This enabled her to unlatch and open it. The instant she did, the wind swung it in to bang against Cullin's inert form.

Anna slipped out, not bothering to pull the door shut again. She swayed across the veranda and stepped off into the snow. The blizzard had tripled its fury in the few minutes since Cullin had carried her inside. On every side the world was muffled in a white, flailing oblivion that beat at her leaning body and roared thunderously in her ears.

Bracing herself, Anna plunged sideways against the slashing snow, her head ducked, her body canted hard to meet the wind's thrust. To her left, she thought. That was the way back to the station. She slogged on for a few yards, having to fight for each step she gained.

After a minute or two? three? she realized it was no good. She was making almost no headway against the wind. Even with her head down, she was half blinded by the stinging blasts of snow. When she raised her head and rubbed her eyes briefly clear, she could still make out nothing.

It was impossible! She was in the center of town somewhere, could not be more than yards from one building or another, yet she couldn't make out even the dim outline of one. She was completely swallowed by the pale, savage gulf of storm.

For the first time apprehension touched her. But she kept her head. She had come only a little distance from the assayer's office. She could make it back there easily, moving with the wind.

Turning back, she was alarmed to find that she could no longer single out the building. But she knew where it was. Taking long plunging steps, she plowed back along the way she thought she had come. At any moment she expected to bark her knees against the veranda. But she found nothing.

Real panic grabbed Anna. It held a chill deeper than any blizzard. She should have reached the building! But if not, then where?

Her bootprints. All she'd had to do was follow them. Yes. She should have done that. Kept her eyes wide open and watched the ground.

She flung herself back into the storm's teeth, retracing her steps. But she had covered some bumpy ground where the blowing snow was still thinned to a couple inches' depth. Already her bootmarks were filling up. A few more steps and she realized with a piercing fright that she could no longer make them out.

Anna halted. She dropped down on her haunches and hunched her back against the wind. It was meager protection. She could no longer feel her fingers. Her toes were going numb. The skin of her cheeks felt sliced by the wind; a spike of pain stabbed into her skull between her eyes.

She could not just sit here and freeze. She had to try for some kind of shelter, anything, even a tree or rock that would break the blizzard's subzero impact. She stumbled to her feet and floundered at right angles to the wind. Surely it lay in this direction, the office. All that had happened was that she had failed to use her eyes and had struck out for it at a wrong angle. The wind was out of the north. Then the office had to be . . .

A horrible thought hit her. Even if she was south of the office, how could she tell how far she might be east or west of it? Confusion seized her. Could she have gotten completely turned around?

Oh, God. It's this direction. It has to be! Try. Try . . . She forced her numbed legs to move. Her sobs were choked back in her throat; tears iced on her lashes.

The wind drove her to her knees. She

stumbled upright, only to fall again. A dry, biting whirl of icy flakes filled her nose and mouth; she was choking, strangling on snow.

With only a dim sense of what she was doing, she began to crawl. It was hard thrusting her way blind through the drifts; the numbness was spreading up from her toes and fingers.

She felt very tired. One by one the threads of her failing will broke. It frightened her at first. But in a few moments even that did not matter very much . . .

Raven and Dolph had braved the mounting violence of the storm to carry Mendez' body out to the stable and lay it beside the frozen corpse of the stockboy, Gabe. They covered both bodies with the same tarpaulin.

Dolph glanced at Raven as they stood in the stable's gloom, the wind rocking and creaking its old timbers. The gaunt Negro had been strangely touched by the experience. For the moment they felt the sober bond of warmth that men did after tackling a grim job together.

"Man, I feel sort of sorry for that preacher . . . doctor . . . whatever's his goddam calling."

"Let's get on back," Raven said. He was thinking of Anna Kosciusko. After he'd left her in the shed, the operation had occupied all his attention for an interval in which he'd lost track of time. The thing might have lasted a half-hour . . . an hour . . . or longer. Anyway he ought to lend her a hand bringing in the wood. Maybe, though, with the storm worsening by the minute, she had already returned to the house.

The two men made a dash back to the station. As they went in and secured the door Laddie came up to Raven.

Aimee Parnell had put the little boy up in the loft before the operation so it wouldn't upset him. Actually, Raven thought wryly, he'd never met a living soul — man, woman, or child — that was less excitable than this five-year-old kid.

He looked up at Raven with those very young, fiercely direct eyes. "Where is my mama?"

Aimee Parnell, her sleeves rolled up, was washing down the trestle table with rags, lye soap, and hot water. Now she rinsed her hands and dried them and came over behind the little boy, laying her hands on his shoulders.

"We are worried, Mr. Raven. Anna

should be back here. The storm is getting so very bad. And just now I look in the annex and your brother is gone . . ."

"What?"

Raven cut the word in like a knife. He looked at Dolph. "You see Cull go out?"

Dolph shrugged. "Didn't see nothing, man. You fetched him one handy clip, and I figured he was laid out good. Then we was all busy with Billy. Hell, I wouldn't of noticed St. Gabe's sweet trumpet right then. That boy could of come right out and gone by us without we —"

Raven had wrenched open the door again after Dolph's first words. And the rest were lost in the roaring wind as he plunged out into the storm.

He hugged the station wall for the several yards to its east corner and then headed for the woodshed in a floundering run through the drifts.

He found the shed door open and banging in the wind. Nobody inside. The ax lay in one corner. There was a fresh yellow trough in one gray board where a long splinter had been chewed out: as if the ax had been flung at it.

Plain enough. But where had he taken her? Not far, Raven reasoned. She was strong; she would fight like a tigress. The only way to subdue her would be to knock her unconscious. In a raging storm how far did you carry the dead weight of a good-sized woman? No farther, probably, than the nearest deserted building that was still reasonably intact.

Raven headed away from the shed, hoping to hell that he had guessed right. He partly shielded his face with his arm as he plunged ahead, straining to make out that building. With all visibility cut off beyond a few feet and his eyes stung half-blind, he had nothing to go on but a sketchy mental picture of the town as he had seen it riding in last night. That and what rough bearings he could take by the direction of wind.

Suddenly the side of a building loomed out of the swirling whiteness inches from his face. The wind slammed his body against it almost before he could cushion the impact with his hands.

Raven worked along the wall toward his right. His boot hit a step. He ascended the veranda and, still holding the wall, located the door.

It stood an inch or so ajar, but when he shoved at it, he felt a resistance. He threw his shoulder to the door and put his weight behind it. As he bulled inside, Cullin toppled away from the door, falling on his back. He'd evidently been crouching there, trying weakly to push it shut.

He crawled laboriously to his hands and knees. "Milt," he mumbled. "Got to help me. Help . . ."

He was a pretty ghastly sight. His face was white and glassy-eyed from cold and shock, smeared with runnels of blood that had also matted his hair. He was apparently half frozen as well as injured. Every movement cost him an agony of effort.

What Raven really saw were the four livid scratches on his cheek.

"Where is she?" Raven's eyes were pitiless as he bent down, grabbed Cullin's collar in both fists, and yanked him half upright. "Goddam your stinking soul. *Where?*"

"Don't know . . . done this to me . . . she . . . goddam bitch . . . *Milt!*"

The last word left him like a broken scream. Raven had simply let go, dropping Cullin on his face.

Pivoting on his heel, Raven went out the door with his brother's cry in his ears. But it was instantly drowned in the roaring tumult of the blizzard.

13

During the blizzard of '81 men had totally lost their bearings while crossing broad streets in the center of towns. Their stiff corpses would turn up yards or feet from buildings they could not see through the driving storm. Raven had heard many such stories. And every one swarmed vividly into his mind. Anna had tried to reach the station, of course. But this had meant heading face-on into the wind. She must have been blown off course, all sense of direction shattered, within seconds of leaving this building. If so, she would logically try to get back to it.

That was all Raven had to go on as he stepped off the porch and slogged into the wind. He was lucky. He'd taken less than a dozen hard-won steps when he saw something dark and sprawling in the snow.

He knelt and turned her over. Her dark lashes flickered; her lips stirred. Except maybe for frostbite, she appeared all right. Deep gouges in the snow behind her showed how she had stumbled, fallen, crawled. She had lain like this for only a few moments or those tracks would be blown over.

Raven tugged her partly upright and lifted her to his shoulders, then wheeled into the wind, tramping steadily. It was bitter going, but he had an easy confidence in his own strength and stamina. He'd never met a man he couldn't shade in those departments.

He did have the fleeting thought that it would be wisest to pack her into the building he'd just quitted. But it was cold as a tomb. He also thought momentarily of Cullin and didn't give a damn. What she needed was a warm fire and a hot drink.

Raven headed back for the roadhouse. He hadn't gone far when the uneasy fact began filtering home that he had overestimated his abilities to cope with the blizzard's ripping fury. He was making slow headway against the wind. Anna's weight seemed to increase with each step he took. His shoulders began to ache. An immense weariness seized his legs. Needing both hands to secure her fast to his back, he was unable to protect his face from the blast of icy pellets slashing at his cheeks and forehead.

The cold was excruciating. He had a scarf tied around his head, another scarf tying down his hat over that, and the wool collar of his mackinaw turned up. Yet his head seemed hammered in a vise of cold. His ears were freezing. He could hardly feel his extremities.

The roar of storm was all around them. He knew that he was heading in roughly the right direction, but he also realized that the erratic wind currents were wrinkling him off a straight line, pushing him fluidly one way, then another.

He was sure that he had enough left to reach the roadhouse. The big worry was that he could easily miss it.

Something black and heavy came rushing at him out of the storm. It was, he saw for one instant, the snapped-off top of a small pine. At the last minute it veered on the sliding air, grazed his shoulder, and hurtled past him.

Raven struggled on, head down. He was no longer tramping heavily; he was plodding as if his legs were weighted. Pain spurted through his shoulders. A drunken stagger touched his stride. *I should have reached it by now. Should have. Keep on. Keep . . .*

His driving, awkward stride blundered him into something hard-edged that rapped his knees. His reflexes were so sluggish that his other leg kept up the blind walk, swung forward, and slammed into the same object. The wind and his momentum and Anna's weight overbalanced him. He crashed full-length on his face.

He raised his head, trying to blink his eyes clear. He was lying on his belly across a porch. Not three feet from his face was a boarded-up door. Not the station, this. But shelter. Anything would do.

Anna's slack weight lay bowed across his back, pinning his shoulders. It took all his remaining strength to raise and slowly turn his shoulders so that he could roll her to one side. He tried to stand then, but the wind was too much.

He made it on hands and knees to the door and found that his numb fingers could get no purchase around the two boards that were nailed crosswise. Slowly, with the awkward care of a man drugged or drunk, he inserted both arms between the door and the boards, wrapped them around the crosspiece, and then threw his weight backward. The boards splintered and tore away from the jamb, leaving their nails still embedded. Raven crashed to the porch on his back.

By now his muscles were so numbed that it took him half a minute to maneuver back to his knees. He fumbled with the latch, half expecting it to be rusted shut. But it raised easily; the door swung in at his touch.

Raven forced himself to a last furious effort, grabbing Anna by the wrists, tugging and jerking her body toward the door a few inches at a time. Finally he had her inside. He shut the door and simply sank down against it and sat that way for a while in a total, drained exhaustion.

Some of the numbness left his body. He climbed painfully to his feet and stared around the huge, drafty room. It might have been a lot of things in its time, but he guessed it had last served as a hotel lobby. In one corner was a clerk's desk and a pigeonhole rack. There was a clutter of broken furniture everywhere he looked. What really took his eye, though, was a huge fieldstone fireplace on one wall. There was also a big, rusty stove in the center of the room, and its piping looked intact.

Raven strode back and forth, working the frozen kinks out of his legs, beating his gloved hands. He felt his quickened blood flailing soft sparks along his arms and legs. He took off his gloves and rubbed his red, stinging hands till feeling came back.

Then he hunted through the smashed furniture for odd pieces that would serve as kindling wood. He heaped them beside the hearth and wadded an old newspaper on the iron dogs and dug out his packet of matches.

Getting the paper lighted was the tricky part. He could still hardly feel his flesh; his hands kept fumbling the task. They moved so slowly that even when he got a match fired, it promptly whiffed out in the constant drafts that swept from a score of jagged chinks where the old wall puncheons had warped and shrunk away from the studs.

Finally Raven took a gamble. He spilled half his matches onto the paper, then struck three more matches with one swipe and dropped them on the paper. The rest erupted with a continual sulphurous flare, spinning off hundreds of sparks, while he shoved in splintered pieces of wood. The blaze took strongly; he piled on larger chunks. His hands tingled and swelled in the warmth.

Among the furniture was a wide leather settee, its cover split and most of the horsehair padding oozed out. Raven dragged it over to the hearth and then carried Anna over and put her down in a sitting position. She was still completely limp, ominously so to his eye. He shook her roughly; her head rolled and she muttered some foreign words.

"Wake up!" He snapped her head back with a hard slap. She began to make little mewing protests.

Snow, seeping from chinks above, had built up in little scattered mounds on the floor by one wall. Raven got a double handful of the cold stuff and rubbed it into her fingers and cheeks. She protested a little more loudly, but her responses were annoyingly like a dreamer's, and she wouldn't open her eyes. He went over her with his big hands, quickly and roughly, massaging her flesh as he would knead dough. This was no damned time for niceties.

Her coat hampered him, so he stripped that off. He relieved her of Cullin's gun and shell belt while he was about it. Her bulky wool skirt and petticoat were also in the way. He raised them rather gingerly to her knees and saw that her decorated boots were caked with melting snow that had gotten down inside the loose tops and soaked her long black stockings.

He took off the boots, then felt to the tops of the firmly gartered stockings and worked them loose and peeled them off. Her legs were long and muscular and beautifully shaped. He rubbed snow over the slender feet and ankles, the hard, rounded calves. At first her flesh was like cold wood under his hands. As warmth came gradually back and she began to stir he felt the smooth, rippling life under the wet, satiny skin.

"Oh," she said.

He hastily quit and jerked her skirts down, then propped her boots and stockings by the fire to dry. Then he gathered up handfuls of the leaked padding from the settee and went around the walls, stopping the chinks one by one with wads of horsehair. Afterward he returned to the fireplace and stood facing it, his palms spread to the fire.

Anna was stirring behind him. She said dully, "My stockings —"

"Were wet." He snapped the words, not looking around.

"Oh."

There was a short silence, except for the avid crackle of flames and their mounting roar in the flue. He heard her slowly move again, as if testing her muscles, and then her soft, excited exclamation. "Oh! Is stove! I must have it over to house."

Raven turned from the fire, eying her with a quiet incredulity.

Anna blushed, but her eyes shone with pleasure at the discovery. "You never cook on open fireplace? No? Then you not know. Is no good. Logs burn through, dishes and food all over floor. I am so sick this mess! Now I have stove."

He couldn't fail to note a faint, rising challenge in her eyes, as though she were both embarrassed and defiant. "Is warmer. You light stove too," she said.

Raven nodded and crossed to the large square stove. He laid paper and wood on the grate and carried a blazing chunk from the fireplace to get it started. In a few minutes, with sources of heat on two sides, the place was a good deal warmer. But the barnlike lobby was still drafty from tatters of wind gusting raggedly through dozens of unseen cracks. Anna kept her coat thrown around her shoulders.

"This is old hotel," she murmured. "You carry me so far?"

"I don't see nobody else around," he said dourly.

There was plenty of room on the settee,

but he stayed standing by the hearth, one arm crooked on the mantel, and stared into the fire. He felt peculiarly ugly and resentful. He wished he were out of the storm anywhere but here.

"Lost my way back to the roadhouse. Stumbled in here." He wanted to make sure she had this very straight.

"Good place as any to wait out the storm."

"Yes." She was quiet a moment; he felt her dark, studying eyes. "Your brother —"

"I saw him. Left him there."

"But I think . . . I kill him."

"You didn't."

"Oh." Another silence. "Is very cold. Maybe he freeze there. Maybe —"

"The hell with him."

"You no mean this?"

He didn't answer. After a moment she said, low-voiced, "I sorry. I am wrong about you. Is no easy to trust. After my husband is kill, there are many men who try bad things. But before there was the Russian officer — who look like you —"

Raven turned his head in surprise. "Like me! What officer?"

"Is man who kill Stephen, my husband."

He looked slowly back at the fire. She went on haltingly. "Is wrong. I know now, you are no like these other men. No like this Shallot and . . . and your brother." A little pause. "But you with them, eh? Why? Is him? Is your brother?"

"Yeah." Raven let his eyes squint nearly shut; flames shimmered between his lids like soft, flowing gold. "I don't know anymore . . . guess for years I figured he'd get over it. Then I knew he wouldn't, but I kept trying. Been that way since —"

He stopped. He had never talked to a woman, really talked; and it seemed vaguely wrong to discuss this family shame.

"Please. You tell me."

He looked at her again and was struck by the mature understanding in her face. What could she know about these things? But she had had her own troubles; they were merely different. Maybe all people in trouble were alike if you dug far enough.

So he told her. Of fighting his brother's fights when they were kids. Of Cullin picking a hundred more fights because he had known Milt would fight them all. And finally of following Cullin into outlawry after he had gone too far — with a girl.

The girl had gotten frightened and screamed and Cullin had used those strong clever hands of his to silence her. Not to kill her, of course. At least, as he told it, he

186

hadn't meant to. And at the time Raven hadn't a thought beyond that dim excuse.

He'd thought of only two things. First, of getting Cullin far away before the body was discovered. Second, of the fact that from this time on, because he was responsible for Cullin's going free, he must stick close to him every hour of every day.

"Figured it didn't matter how he was, long as I was around to control him. Worked out for a long time. Seemed to." Slowly he shook his head. "Don't seem it did, though. Or this with you wouldn't of happened. All my doing. There's places to put people like him away. That's where he belongs."

"But . . . you too hard on yourself, no? Is your brother!"

"No damned excuse. Reckon it's all the worse. Man don't want to look at rot in his kin. Afraid it might be in his own blood."

"No. Is not so!" Anna shook her head vigorously. "I had aunt who was . . . strange. Very young, she was put away. Then we no talk of her. Maybe we all be afraid, eh? But then we all be alike too."

They talked off and on for hours. Raven replenished the fires from time to time. The silences were pleasant, odorous with

187

the smell of the old musty building and the wood smoke and the damp clothes drying.

Anna did most of the talking. But as time went along she talked less and less. She kept watching him intently, her eyes warmed by little kindling lights. His imagination, he supposed. Or the play of firelight.

A drowsy warmth stole through him as he crouched on the hearth with his arms wrapping his legs. His face settled by degrees against his knees; he dozed. He jerked awake and glanced around. Anna was sitting exactly as she had been. Her eyes were gentle and reproving and amused.

"So tough you are." Her words were gibing, but her tone was not.

"Better go to sleep."

"So. Then, you come off cold hearth. Here." She patted the settee beside her. "For warmth. Do not be foolish, eh? There is not so much wood. Is long night ahead. Maybe longer storm."

He eased stiffly to his feet. She stretched out on the settee on her side and cramped herself against its back to make room for him. He lay down in a very gingerly way, putting his back to her.

Gradually their clothing warmed from the heat of their bodies and with slow insistence, though she did not move, her body made a specifically molded shape against his, the warm firmness of her thighs roundly pressing, the two solid cones swelling against his back. She laughed softly in his ear.

"Something funny?"

"I think how strange," she whispered. "I hate a man so. Now to think I owe him all. Everything, eh?"

"That was plain duty. After my brother —"

"You no say that," she said sharply. "No say it again. No think it anymore." She paused, then very softly said, "You no tough at all."

After a small eternity of lying there, just wondering, he felt her hand slip up and under his arm and around his shoulder.

Even then it seemed so strange that he wasn't sure. But he turned himself to her and felt her arms open and take him in. Her mouth had a sweet fruitlike flavor. Her strong hands were quick and gentle in their touchings. She moaned and hugged him tighter, arching her body against him.

14

Darkness came but was hardly noticed. The blizzard howled through the night. Dolph Smith knew it was letting up some when he could peer out the door and make out a vague suggestion of false dawn. He braved the still-bitter violence of the storm to fetch some cedar from the woodshed. He found a good-sized scatter of freshly split length around the chopping block, but no sign thereabouts of Anna Kosciusko or the Raven brothers.

He made three trips from the house and back, half filling the kitchen woodbox. Chilled to his marrow by then, Dolph hastily got a roaring blaze going. As soon as his teeth had quit chattering, he measured Triple X into a big cow-camp coffeepot, filled it with water, and hung it on a trammel pothook. He slapped a thick, barely thawed elk steak into a skillet and propped it on the logs, then dug into the sourdough crock for biscuit makings.

From the common room came the arguing of the two Parnells. They had been at it off and on for hours. The preacher had been dipping into Cernak's white mule, despite his wife's remonstrations.

"What do you care?" he was saying thickly. "You know you married a coward. Knew it long before you told Raven so."

"Oh, James," she said wearily. "How many times must I say it? I am so sorry for that."

"Don't be. We are told the truth shall make ye free. That's what we're told."

"But it wasn't the truth, James! You are not a coward. Did you not marry a Catholic girl from New Orleans? A stranger to your city, your people, even your religion? You stood against your family, your friends, even your congregation — told them all they could go hang for bigots. That was a brave thing. And how proud I was of you!"

"Brave? That was such a damned little thing. And you didn't even know about . . . all that before —"

"But I know now. *Mon cher,* you let one mistake change your life! I think that was foolish, not cowardly. Then you could not forgive yourself, so you would not believe that anybody else could, even God —"

Parnell hammered his fist on the table. "Don't you understand? I'm not real! Nothing about me is real! I'm no surgeon — never could be. One man died because I thought I was. One lesson wasn't enough — now I've done it again —"

"Oh, that is stupid! How can you say —"

Dolph shook his head in awe as he flopped the soft mass of sourdough on the sinkboard and chunked it into pieces. These quality white people were the goddamndest caution ever a man saw. No matter how upset things got, they never let it out in a blue yell with some good, healthy cussing. Did they, things would look a heap brighter.

Dolph greased the biscuits and dropped them in the biscuit pan and set it on the logs; then he forked the sizzling steak over. Afterward he stepped to the doorway and cleared his throat.

" 'Scuse me, white folks. You want something to eat?"

The Reverend Mr. Parnell sat dull and haggard-eyed, nursing a cup between his hands. His wife sat across from him. Both glanced at Dolph. *Can't you see we're suffering?* their tired, reproachful looks seemed to say. *Hell,* Dolph thought, *who ain't?*

"You ought to eat something, Doc."

"No, nothing. Thank you."

"You, Missus?"

Aimee Parnell shook her head miserably. She stood now and skirted the table and slid her arm around her husband's shoulder. "Come, James. Come now, you must get some sleep . . ."

Unprotesting, numbly docile, he permitted her to draw him to his feet and leaned his weight heavily on her as they went into the annex.

Dolph clucked his tongue, feeling (in spite of himself) sorry for the preacher. Suddenly he heard a flaky thud, a clatter of falling pans, a sizzle of grease. He wheeled back into the kitchen and looked at the fireplace. A burning log had collapsed, tumbling flaming chunks on the hearth and upending the biscuit pan in the ashes. The soft, greased biscuits were mired in soot. The spider was knocked over too, the skillet overturning in the ashes with Dolph's steak.

"Lousy sonofabitching white man's fireplace!" Dolph fetched the biscuit pan a kick that sent it whanging against the wall.

The hell with it. He wasn't hungry anyway. The coffee was boiling and it would go just right with some of that white man's hell brew.

He carried the coffeepot and two cups out to the trestle table, filled one cup from the rotgut keg at the bar, and returned to the table. He took turns swigging the tarry coffee and the pale liquor. The mixture curled like hot wires around his entrails.

Dolph shivered as he listened to the storm whistling dismally around the eaves. Jesus, but he hated that sound. Made him think of the leaky barn of that Georgia redneck who had inherited them from well-to-do kin, him and his pa and ma, and had sold them away from him. ("Hesh you big bawlin' mouth, boy. Po' man cain't feed but one nigra, and you pap and mam, they ailin'.") Of course it wasn't always cold, but it seemed that cold times were all he could remember in that thin-walled barn where he'd had to sleep, chill winds cutting through the cracks all night. Dreams of hot, golden sunshine curling around his belly, his limbs. Ah, God!

The hell with that too. After this, his share of the loot pocketed, he was breaking with that fine Southern gentleman Captain Shallot. No more back-door blackbirding in a mean white man's world for this nigger. Not deep in Mexico, where a man was no more low-down than any other with a fortune in his poke.

He wondered some about the fate of the Raven boys and the Polack girl. They had frozen or they had taken cover in another building. Either way, all he could do was wait.

Aimee Parnell came from the annex and crossed into the kitchen and the little adjoining room, where the boy was still asleep. Dolph heard Laddie's sleep-querulous voice, a plaintive note in it. Tough little kid, but he was worried too . . .

Dolph hesitated before taking another double swallow of coffee and booze. He guessed he could afford to loosen his vigilance. The driver was still asleep from the beating Albie had fetched him nearly twenty-four hours ago and he didn't look as if he'd ever wake up. Albie, sick and feverish with his bad hand, had gone back to the annex and his bunk hours ago. The preacher and his wife would make no trouble.

Dolph's head came up. What was that feeble thumping sound?

At first he'd thought the wind. Now he thought it might be somebody pounding softly and weakly on the outside door. He got up and unbarred and opened it.

Cullin was there, crumpled down on his knees. It must have taken every ounce of effort he could muster to tap the door with his fist. Dolph bent and hauled him to his feet and half dragged him over to a chair by the closest fireplace . . .

It was some time before Cullin, revived by generous doses of rotgut and hot coffee, could manage a gravelly whisper. He gave Dolph a sketchy and profane idea of what had happened.

Dolph wondered that Cull was still alive. Huddled in the blanket Dolph had brought him, he looked like plain hell. His hair was clotted with blood from great, raw gashes, and his face looked as if he had met a baby tiger. His skin, a corpselike white-blue when Dolph had pulled him inside, was just starting to warm to a frostbitten mottled hue.

". . . had to stay in that goddam place all night." He had trouble forming speech; his lips stuttered woodenly. "Cold . . . freezing all goddam night. Had to keep moving . . . keep alive. Couldn't come back here till storm dropped off enough. Hardly made it then."

"Seems you purely got what you asked for," Dolph said. "What about Milt? The Polack gal?"

"How the hell would I know? Froze for all I know. If they didn't and they show up . . ." Cullin shook his head very slowly, a lusty sheen on his eyes. "Jesus. Will I make them two sorry."

He lurched to his feet, stood swaying a moment, then tossed the blanket aside. He went in a stumbling, stiff-legged wobble over to the miscellaneous arms stacked in the corner. He chose Cernak's old Colt and checked the loads and rammed it in his belt, muttering to himself. Then he moved to the bar, hooked his elbows on its edge, and filled a cup to the brim with rotgut.

Dolph went back to the table and sat down. Uneasy, he watched Cullin slug down drink after drink. Crazy goddam fool. Well, no concern of his. Keeping purely out of white-man business was how a blackbird kept his wings from getting clipped. Blackbird, he learned how to fly young.

The moaning wind was no lullaby, but it had a kind of even monotony that deadened a tired man's nerves, even Dolph Smith's restless, quivering ones. He finished his rotgut and coffee. After a while he settled his head on his arms.

Shallot stood in the tunnel mouth, shivering, and watched the cold, false-dawn light grow. His eyes were vicious, and he swore, not caring whether Terrill heard him or not. The blizzard had died down to slow, raw gusts, and the air was growing colder.

Cernak, he thought, would have found shelter as soon as the storm had gotten too severe for him to press on safely. But the worst of it was past. By now Cernak would be leaving his refuge, pushing on down the mountain to Thirty Mile.

Shallot turned back into the tunnel, retreating to the fire a few yards inside its mouth. The flames whipped like angry banners in the wind. He'd had a time getting it started, had managed it with a few handfuls of dry resinous twigs he'd gathered from the bases of conifers growing a little ways downslope. He had kept the fire high and roaring by a constant stoking with loose pieces of timber he had scrounged from the old mine works.

Now he threw on a couple more chunks and crouched facing the warmth, palms out, warming his face and hands.

Quintus Terrill lay just beyond the fire on a makeshift bed of old timbers and some sacking Shallot had found in a shack. He'd made Quintus as comfortable as could be and had partly stanched the flow of blood. But he knew it was hopeless.

Cernak's bullet must have hit the spine. Quintus couldn't move his legs. Not that it would matter in a while. Quintus was gutshot, his life hemorrhaging away slowly. Very slowly.

His face was grayish. His eyes were bright and faraway; he faintly smiled, as if listening to a lost long-ago voice. But he was quite rational.

"Good old George," he whispered. "We both know what's in your head, don't we? Same old George."

"Quit it, Quintus."

"Now the storm's let up, he'll be moving on fast, won't he? Every minute that passes, he's pulling farther away. And you're stuck here, waiting on me to cash a busted chip."

"I could leave you to freeze."

"Sure you could." Terrill began to laugh. But the laughter squeezed off at once; his face rippled with a spasm of pain. "Christ," he gasped. "How things work out, eh? I mean, if the Polack had just killed me outright. Or if I could move enough to keep the fire built up . . . you could leave me. You could tell yourself I'd be all right till you got back. But this — ha ha . . ."

"Maybe," Shallot said thinly, "you'll just laugh yourself to death, Quintus."

Restlessly he got to his feet and paced back and forth, biting his lip in a gray fury. He thought of Cernak reaching the station. Well-armed. In a passion to free his daughter, his grandson.

Could he? Fifty-fifty, Shallot thought grimly. Albie was stupid. Cullin, unreliable and erratic. Both Raven and Dolph were smart and alert. But that might not count for much if Cernak put those weasely peasant wits of his to work. Besides, he'd have the element of surprise in his favor.

Shallot hadn't admitted to himself till now how important the recovery of the money had been to him. The wasting thing in his system hadn't destroyed his desire for life, only his zest for it. How much time had he left? Months? Or years? He didn't know. But he knew how he wanted to spend them. At utter ease in soft tropic warmth, waited on hand and foot. The one last job, the big money — and it had slipped through his fingers . . .

"You were right, George, all along," Terrill husked. "Everything is a lie. No reason for honor. Friendship. For anything. So why can't you leave me?"

Shallot continued to slowly pace, not

even glancing at him.

"I'll tell you why. You're a sucker, George. You're tied to a handful of ragged memories. Boyhood chums. Old time's sake. It may be the only human feeling you have left, but there it is. Just another dreamer, George, eh?"

"Quintus, why don't you shut up?"

"Presently. Very presently. I just wanted to add, you're not only a sucker, old boy, you're a liar too. You've proved it to yourself. Now I'm going to prove it again."

Some note in his tone made Shallot turn his head sharply. Terrill's fist held a tiny pistol, a gambler's spare he'd always carried in an inside pocket.

"I'm going to make it easy for you, George."

"Quintus —" Shallot said wildly.

The gun turned against Terrill's coat. Before Shallot could move even a muscle, the gun made a muffled, whip-snap bark.

Shallot had started around the fire. He halted, staring down, as the echoes died. *You goddam fool, Quintus. I would have stayed by. I would have . . .*

The thought threaded away even as it formed. His thoughts were turning back to the money. And the need for haste.

15

"So strange," Anna murmured. "I hated you so. Now is all different. Is like I know you forever. How is this?"

"Read a book once. Said that love and hate are pretty near the same."

She laughed. "Now you talk silly."

They lay close together on the settee, and her head was pillowed on his shoulder. The wind continued outside; the stove's cooling metal made a measured ticking in the room. Raven felt her move and her weight shift a little away, and opened his eyes. She had raised her body so that her head bent above his.

She smiled with tenderness, touching his cheek. "Lucifer, he have such a face after The Fall."

"He was worse off'n I thought."

"No. Is a beautiful face made terrible. That is what I mean."

"Afraid I got born with this one."

Anna leaned deeper. Her loosened hair veiled their heads. Her lips nibbled over his face in the kisses of afterlove, brief, tender, grateful. She laid her face against the side of his neck, quiet again.

It was still hard for him to believe. Women in his life had always been the whores in some lousy crib that Cullin would drag him into, everything seen through an alcohol haze (brittle-bright and slurred at the edges and quickly fading in the recesses of memory, but maybe he had never wanted to remember). He had not believed it could happen as a natural, artless surrender to physical need, and be beautiful. Now he knew it could. Admittedly if the need hadn't been overwhelming for both, it wouldn't have happened this way, this soon. But there was still far more here than the physical.

Anna had said it as they had talked together through the long stormy night hours. She had talked of many things — little tender snatches of recollection that had thronged back after this melting of hard defenses that she had built against the world. Memories of childhood holidays, of dancing the mazurka and the oberek, of sleigh rides and tinkling bells and icy air ringing with childish laughter, of windowpanes tracked with silvery whorls and delicate white ferns of frost.

"On the Sabbath," she had murmured, "we would go to church and pray our dear Poland be no longer the bone to be chewed over by Russians, Austrians, Prussians. But we no remember when it was different. Even the very old, they no remember. But in the church is peaceful. And the snow, we come out, the snow fall so soft. I think of that, now is snow fall."

Raven had chuckled a little. "I reckon this is what church is supposed to keep folks out of."

Her laughter had rippled, a quiet glissando. "But I feel like in church. If is bad, God no let me feel that way." She had been very serious about this.

They had talked of other things. "My husband was brave man. I want Ladislas not forget this, to remember his father always so. This you see?"

"Sure. Boy should have a good memory of his real pa. Only right that he should."

That part, too, had been a natural and accepted thing — that their two lives were now one and that her son would share that oneness. But Laddie would have his own life too.

Raven had done more than turn his back

on Cullin. He had filled Cullin's place with something bigger and better. And that realization had changed everything else too.

As the wintry blasts continued to hammer against the house, they slept. Raven came awake to Anna's hand gently shaking his arm. His eyes questioned her.

"Is getting light," she whispered. "Wind is no so bad now, I think."

Raven swung to his feet and crossed the old lobby to the door. He opened it. The wind smote his face like an icy blow, yet it had eased off considerably. The driving snow had thinned too, so that he could make out near objects. He was surprised to see that the night had come and gone; a dirty gray glow of dawn had advanced across the whole world.

"Reckon we can make it back to the house now."

"But first we have plan, no?"

He nodded and shut the door and went back to the fireplace, where the coals had crumbled to glowing red eyes. He tossed in a dry chunk and watched it blaze up.

"I no care how we do it," Anna said, watching his face. "Just so my boy no hurt."

"I care," Raven said quietly. "I rode by these men a long way, Anna. We'll see your boy gets out safe. But I don't want to have to fight 'em unless need be."

"But if you need to?" She walked slowly over to him. "Milt!"

She felt a clear anxiety as to how his loyalty would turn if he were faced with a choice. The swollen side of her face was darkly discolored in the muddy light. He lifted his hand and touched her chin very gently below the swelling.

"Sure. If I need to. Don't worry."

Cernak had waited out the whole night in the cramped gorge, sheltered from the blizzard and fairly pocketed from the intense cold. When the storm had started to let up in the still-murky dawn, he crawled out of the narrow cleft, so stiff with cold that he could hardly move his muscles. He felt almost detached from his arms and legs. He stood on the rim for a few minutes, shuffling up and down in an ungainly dance, beating his hands together. It got his blood up and warmed him back slowly to a living presence. He felt real again, blood and flesh and bone.

During the long, chill, unmoving hours his hot thoughts had cooled drastically. The more he had considered, the more he realized the foolhardiness of any try to revenge himself on the gang.

He had settled Shallot's hash, he was reasonably sure. The rest? They'd only done Shallot's bidding. He had no interest in them, nor they in him, beyond the money. That was the only real stake any of them had in this affair. And he had the money. What else did he need?

Nothing but getting Anna and Laddie out of the station and away from Thirty Mile. Not that he had any compunctions about killing any or all of them if he had to. But they outnumbered him — Dolph and Albie and the two Ravens. Why take a chance on getting killed himself?

His best chance was to trick them. Somehow. He had no firm ideas, but his shrewd brain was ferreting out every possibility as he did up the fastenings of his snowshoes and stomped up and down to make sure they were on securely.

Cernak made good time on the drifted trail coming down the tapering sweep of peak flank. The wind had kept the snow pared to a thin level on the higher places, tending to drift it always into the low and valleyed areas. He could have moved pretty fast even without snowshoes, Cernak realized.

The trouble was, then so could Shallot.

He had hoped the snow would deepen enough to greatly slow Shallot when he tried to get off the mountain — probably maroon him. Now Cernak knew that it wouldn't. He guessed that Shallot could make it out in maybe a couple of hours.

But Cernak did not quicken his pace. He had to be reasonably fresh, when he reached Thirty Mile, to do what he must. He moved at a strong, sweeping stride along the trail rim, wary of firm-looking snow ledges that brinked out over the plunging drop. He lost no time, but he let his feet instinctively feel every step before his weight came down fully.

Meantime the dawn was growing. The murky pale had spread across the whole sky, and the wind was falling off steadily. The snow had let up too. The temperature had dropped by a few degrees, and he hoped it wouldn't get too much colder. If he got Anna and Laddie out safely, they still faced a long journey.

At last he dropped down the final leg of trail above Thirty Mile. Below him the buildings were an untidy sprawl, like up-ended and scattered matchboxes on the smooth white floor of the pass. Knowing he could be easily spotted on the pale mountain wall, Anton left the open trail.

He chose a way down that would keep him behind or close to the finger-shaped mottes of dark pine that straggled upward from the lower slope.

It took him a long time to make it this way, zigzagging often so as not to expose himself on the open stretches. When he finally reached the edge of Thirty Mile, full dawn had poured into the pass. It was quite light now, and the falling snow had slacked off to where he could pick out details nearly as well as on any clear day.

As he'd expected, the snow was not nearly as deep down here as anybody would think who did not know this pass. It tended to pile up steeply where the gorge walls began but stayed quite thin out toward the center. Something about the way that the walls tipped air currents down in sharp-blowing slashes that gusted rain or sleet or snow off along the sides. A stage or wagon couldn't make it in or out, but a man on horseback could all winter long if he hung to the direct center of the pass.

Good. He had the plan now.

Staying where he was behind one of the old sheds but standing a little back from it, he had a good vantage of the whole town. His roadhouse stood about midway between the east and the west ends, with a string of deserted buildings running to either side.

The livery barn was well to the east of the roadhouse. His problem was to get Anna and Laddie out of the station and across to the barn — and the horses. Then they'd head with all speed for Saintsburg, which was at least seven miles nearer than Silverton.

The idea had seemed thin at first, but the more he thought about it, the more feasible it seemed. If the men in the roadhouse could be distracted for only a few minutes, they would have a chance.

After discarding his snowshoes he slipped along behind the buildings until he was directly opposite the livery barn. He made a short, hard dash across the street, lifting his knees in high, stabbing steps through the snow. For a few seconds he was in plain sight of the station, but there was little chance anybody would look out just then.

Cernak swung the bar off its brackets, then let himself into the musty barn. The horses stood hipshot and heads down. A few glanced sleepily out of their stalls and didn't seem interested. He tramped down the runway, halting as he passed a stall, where he noticed a tarp covering something inside. He stepped over and raised the tarp. Of course. Gabe. And he felt no surprise at seeing Mendez laid out alongside. The Mexican's leg had been taken off, and there it was beside him, wrapped up neat as a butcher's package.

Cernak moved quickly now, saddling and bridling his two best horses. He tied them to a stall post close to the door so that he and Anna could mount and break away fast. He could carry the boy in front of him.

Maybe there wouldn't be time, but if there was, he could drive all the horses out ahead of them, leaving four men afoot and cut off from any possibility of pursuit.

Leaving the barn now, he circled back behind the buildings on this side. He skirted along their rear at a broad, plunging trot through the snow, going boldly past the roadhouse, which had no windows toward its back. He came to the last building on the west outskirt, a tack shed that was all but falling apart. The sagging door hung open. He stepped inside and jammed it shut.

The dirt floor was scattered with loose scraps of lumber. Cernak swept them with his fingers into a single pile, then took out his matches. The wind whistling through numerous cracks made it hard to get a bit of bark ignited. Once he had it going, he carefully shielded the flame with his body and fed it more bark, then small sticks. He didn't want a big, roaring blaze. He wig-wammed medium-small pieces over the fire, enough to keep it going awhile.

He opened the loading gates of both pistols, his own and Terrill's, and found that each contained three unspent cartridges. After a moment's hesitation he stripped Terrill's gun of its three shells and laid them on a thin, narrow slab of wood. This he set with infinite care across the fire.

For a moment he crouched, cupping the fire between his big, callused palms as it grew. When the thin blue strands of smoke began curling up from the slab's edges, he grinned crookedly. It would take, all right.

Rising, he opened the door, stepped out quickly, and again jammed it shut. Then he cut back the way he had come, running along back of the buildings till he came to several stacks of lumber, unused and rotting, behind the old feed company store.

Anton sank down on his haunches between two tiered heaps of boards. From here he had a perfect view of the roadhouse. He waited, his heart pounding. He would not have to wait long.

16

Dolph dreamed he was back in the redneck's Georgia shanty. He was seven years old on a warm, humid blue-bottle-fly sort of summer afternoon. He playing in the dust by the steps and his mama singing one of her sweet, high, happy-sad chants in the kitchen as she worked. His daddy and the white man working in the fields. The white man appearing suddenly, tramping across the clearing into the kitchen *("Now, nigra, you be good")* and his mama starting to scream.

Dolph groaned and twisted in his chair. His arms, pillowing his head, now unwrapped and scrabbled sideways till his long fingers gripped the edge of the table and squeezed. This was a dream, he knew it was, he had to wake, to pull himself up from the dismal, sickly wool of sleep —

He jerked awake.

He raised his head, sweat oozing from every pore. He was really awake now. Yet the screaming did not stop. It continued to fill his ears, above the continuing moan of wind, above even the ringing ache in his skull.

There was a foul taste in his mouth too. He had drunk too much — and now he had slept for hours in an awkward position. Also he was stiff from cold; the fires had gone out. The unnatural gray light that filled the room told him that it was nearly full dawn. The lowering wind said that the storm had tapered off . . .

Suddenly Dolph, his brain working like molasses, groggily realized that the screams were real. They were coming from the annex.

He glanced quickly at the bar. Cullin had been standing there drinking when Dolph had dropped off. He was gone now — maybe staggered back to the annex to sleep it off. Or do something else.

Dolph knocked over his chair, coming to his feet. Lunging around the table, he went down the passage to the annex at a run.

The curtain that divided the annex room had been pushed aside. The Reverend James Parnell was stretched out on the floor, unconscious. His lady wife lay crumpled on her face by one wall. Cullin was kneeling beside her. The upper parts of her dress and camisole hung in shreds around her waist; Cullin was fumbling with her skirt.

Albie stood by watching, his eyes shining, low-pitched giggles bubbling in his throat. Then he glanced toward Dolph. His mirth choked off.

Cullin looked up quickly. Seeing Dolph, he took his hands away from the woman. A returning sanity cooled his eyes. Never taking his eyes off Dolph, he came slowly to his feet. His right hand inched toward his gun.

"Nigger, you better back outa here. Ain't no sight here for your woolly eyes."

"Shut up!"

Dolph snarled the words, at the same time slapping his hand over his gun butt and whipping the .45 up, cocked and leveled. He caught Cullin square in the middle of his draw.

Cullin might be crazy, but he was no fool. He froze still, and Dolph crossed to him and took the gun away and shoved it in his own belt. Then he motioned both of them over against the wall.

A kind of sick dread filled Dolph as he glanced down at the still form of the woman. For a moment all he could see was white flesh. Naked white-woman flesh.

The vomit clawed up in his throat. For the first time he was facing what every black man feared most, a clammy, unreasoning fear taken almost with his mother's milk.

Dolph raised his eyes, a muscle leaping in his jaw as he pointed the .45 at Cullin and Albie. "You bastards. You stinking sonsabitches. You know what you two done involved me in? White-woman business. Black man gets touched by white-woman business, he's good as dead! By Jesus God, I ought to kill the both o' you here and now!"

"You going to?" Albie whimpered.

"Naw," Dolph said thickly. "Too late now. Shoulda been done before ever you two got started. Done now, and these two, they'll swear to it." He motioned at the two unconscious people. "You goddam fools, you likely swing for this. Likely. But me, I'm dead for sure —"

"That don't follow," Albie said.

"I was here!" Dolph yelled. His eyes stung with fury. "You goddam nit-brain, don't you know that's enough?"

"Look," Cullin said softly. "You ain't thinking. No reason they got to tell anyone."

Dolph was already shaking his head with a deadly, flat emphasis. "One thing you don't do, boy. You don't kill no man of God. His lady wife neither. I done a lot of things that red devil will make me fry for, but I ain't sunk that far." A fresh rage poured through him. "By God, I'm minded to do for you bastards anyways."

Cullin stood blinking at him, his face slack and whiskey-bloated and brutal. Dolph wondered in that moment why he had ever thought that Milt Raven was the ugly one of the two.

"What the hell," Cullin said sullenly then. "I didn't do nothing. Peeled a couple things off her was all."

"You a goddam liar. You slugged her cold —"

"Hell I did! She fainted."

Dolph was skeptical, but he looked again, this time more carefully. The woman's shoulders were marked by livid abrasions, but maybe these were caused when her clothes were ripped away, sawing her tender skin. The skirt of her dress had been torn too, but her petticoats were intact. Apparently Cullin really hadn't gotten any further. And she didn't look to be hurt otherwise.

Dolph's guts felt easier. He had let his own fear, his deepest fear, paralyze him. Even now, though the lady shouldn't be left lying so on the chilly floor, he couldn't assist her. Let it get out that he'd touched a half-naked white lady, no matter what the reason, and she might as well have been beaten and raped after all, for all the difference it would make to a white-man jury. She was a nice sort, but Nawleans gentry too — and Dolph was taking no chances.

He walked over to a bunk, stripped off a blanket, and chucked it at Albie. "Pick the lady up. Put her in the bunk yonder. See you wrap that blanket around her first."

Albie awkwardly did as he was told. The preacher began groaning on the floor. Dolph knelt and turned Parnell's head and saw the dark, spreading welt on his temple, made, no doubt, by a pistol laid across his skull when he had come to his wife's defense. His unshaven face was stained a sickly pallor, but he should come around all right.

Straightening, Dolph motioned Cullin and Albie to move ahead of him out of the annex. They tramped sullenly back to the common room.

"Seems I just got to keep an eye on you —" Dolph began saying, when a shot echoed from outside.

The three of them halted just inside the common room. They gave each other blank looks, and then Cullin said, "Better see what that was."

"You wait awhile. Listen."

Cullin's lip curled. His cockiness was coming back. "Don't get the idea we're taking orders from no shithouse nigger all at once."

Dolph simply flipped his gun from his right hand to his left, then backhanded Cullin across the mouth. The blow was so hard that it swiveled Cullin's head. Blood spurted from his lip. He dropped back a step, his jaw falling.

"You taking 'em from this one, boy," Dolph said.

He saw the pale shock and fury in Cullin's face, and it made him feel good. He laughed. It was the first time he had laughed in a long, long while. He felt a rush of pure exuberance. He kept laughing in his throat, soft and easy.

"I ain't no low-chip badman like you," he told Cullin. "I'm a mean canebrake nigger who got weaned off a hard-liquor tit. I'm a black bull 'gator and a son of a bitch, and ain't no man crosses me but once. Far as I'm concerned, you had your once. Take heed."

On the heel of his words, there was a solid roar of gunfire from somewhere on the street. It began and ended just that suddenly.

Dolph listened for another moment, then strode to the corner where the weapons were stacked. He scooped up the stockboy's shotgun and a couple boxes of shells. He broke the gun and inserted two loads and snapped the breech shut.

"Now we gonna see what that's about," he announced. "Cull and me going down the street, Albie. You stay and mind the store."

Albie nodded a prompt understanding. A plain-out order always found his dull brain quick and receptive.

Dolph tugged Cullin's gun from his belt and tossed it to him. Cullin caught it and balanced it in one hand. He rubbed his other hand gently over his jaw, watching Dolph.

"You bought it now," he whispered. "I don't take it off no niggers. You watch it."

"All I plan on watching is you, boy," Dolph grunted. "You look wrong at me once, just once, and I bust you before you bat a winker. I can outmove you without I half try. You know it. Now, get out that door ahead of me. Anyone waiting out there to bust us, you might's well find it out first. Move along there, boy."

★ ★ ★

The simple plans were the best ones, Raven said. They would return to the roadhouse easily and casually, he and Anna; they would tell the simple truth about being cut off by the storm. Then Raven would seize his first chance and get the drop on Dolph and Albie. With those two tied up and out of the way, they could wait strategically for Shallot and Terrill to return with her father — get the drop on them with no trouble.

"But there be other trouble," Anna worried. "My papa, he want this money very bad. This no must be! We must give money back."

"We'll turn it over to the law," Raven told her. "Time enough later to figure all that out. Right now . . ."

Right now he wanted a look inside the old assayer's office. He dreaded what he might find. Cullin had been injured and half frozen. Furious as he'd been, he knew now that he wouldn't have abandoned Cullin to death by freezing, except that saving Anna had come first.

And he knew that Anna, though she'd said nothing, must harbor an equally deep concern for her father. She wasn't the kind to wholly repudiate her own kin, no matter how she felt about him now. When Raven thought about it, he was glad she wasn't.

A damned foolishness too. You knew that they were no good, that they'd throw over anybody, even those closest to them, to get what they wanted. Crazy or plain bad, what did it matter? You were ashamed of them, ashamed of yourself for your weakness, yet you couldn't act otherwise.

Anna was watching his face. She said suddenly, "You worry for him. You *do* worry!"

Raven nodded.

She laid a hand on his wrist with a soft smile of triumph — or relief. "Then, we go see first, eh?"

"You stay here," Raven said grimly. "I'll have a look. Don't step out of here till I get back. Promise me."

She gave a little, reluctant nod.

Raven opened the door and went out into the gray morning. He was surprised at how fast the storm was dying away. The wind was very low; a few cold flakes spiraled against his face. Everything was muffled in a bright, solid whiteness.

He looked down to the end of the street, surprised at how far he was from the roadhouse. He hadn't thought he'd missed the place by so much. His sense of direction in the storm had got squared around hindside-to; the wind must have been changing all the time.

He tramped upstreet toward the assayer's office, his boots crunching the deep fresh snow.

He came to a sudden stop, staring at an areaway between two buildings. Was he seeing things, or had he spotted a man hurrying along back of those buildings? The alley was so narrow that the running figure had crossed it in a split second.

It was worth being sure of. Raven headed down the areaway at a high-kneed lope, breaking through the snow that had banked deeply between the two buildings. He reached the end of the areaway and veered to his right.

The running man had disappeared. But his deep tracks led away at an angling run that cut back of the roadhouse itself and ran beyond. Raven followed the trail, seeing it skirt around behind some long piles of stacked lumber.

Running full-tilt around the ends of the tall stacks, he saw a man crouched at the other end in the space between two of the piles. A squat, massive figure of a man who came swiftly up off his haunches, pivoting around at the same time. His gun swung up.

"Cernak!" Raven threw out his hand. "Wait a minute!"

17

Cernak didn't wait even a second. He simply brought his gun up and fired. Raven spun around and fell on his face in the snow. He didn't move. Cautiously, Cernak tramped over to him and prodded him with a toe. Raven's hat had been ripped by the bullet, knocked askew under the scarf that held it on. Cernak could see that he was bleeding from the scalp, but that was all he could tell.

Maybe he had shot too quickly. This big, gaunt, hawkfaced man was the best of Shallot's bad lot. He hadn't had his gun out, and it would have been as easy to hear him out, then shoot if necessary. But he had been keyed up; he'd shot without considering.

The brief regret crossed his mind in the fleeting part of a second; then he was wheeling back to his position between the lumber stacks. Crouching down where he could see the roadhouse.

Cernak's heart thudded in his chest. Damn it! Would that shot bring the men in the roadhouse right to him? Why in hell hadn't his decoy bullets gone off?

Then the crash of fire-touched gunpowder came from downstreet. Cernak felt a gust of relief. That should fetch them out — and pull them in the wrong direction. *Come on, you bastards!*

The door of the station slammed open. Cullin Raven stumbled out, gun in hand. He was followed closely by Dolph Smith. The two men skirted the station at a half trot, vanishing around the corner. Good. They were heading away from him, toward the source of the shots.

Of the gang, that left Albie unaccounted for. Was he in the roadhouse? Probably. Dolph was too smart not to see that one man remained on guard.

But Cernak couldn't delay. The reason for the shots would baffle Dolph and Cullin for a few minutes. He had to get in and out of the station before they realized how they'd been tricked.

Cernak left the lumber pile now and cut away at a quick run toward the roadhouse but not toward the main door. He moved along the back, reached the kitchen door, and grasped the latch, carefully testing it.

Not locked. The latch raised at his touch, and now he eased open the heavy door with infinite care. The wind was still blowing strongly enough to smother the soft creak of hinges.

Holding the door an inch ajar, Cernak peered in. He could see through the kitchen and the open doorway connecting it to the common room.

As he'd hoped and expected, Albie did not have the sense to put himself where he could watch both doors. He sat stiffly alert at the trestle table, his broad back to the kitchen, his eyes fixed on the main door alone.

He had to subdue Albie as quietly as possible, Cernak thought. A shot would bring back the other two at once.

Slowly, very slowly, Cernak edged the door farther open. A draft, or the increased noise of the wind, alerted Albie then. He started to heave around in his chair.

Cernak moved with an incredible lumbering speed. Five springy strides carried him across the kitchen and into the common room. He reached Albie just as the latter, on his feet now, wheeled around clumsily, grabbing for his belted pistol with his good left hand.

Cernak kicked Albie's chair out of the

way and closed his hand over Albie's good wrist, squeezing with a massive power. His other hand went for Albie's throat. Albie started a yell that Anton's fingers choked down to a feistlike yelp.

Anton used his weight to bend Albie backward across the table. Albie, strong as a young bull, was handicapped by his wounded hand. With it he could only paw futilely, painfully at the powerful throttling fingers around his throat.

Abruptly Cernak let go of Albie's wrist, slammed his hand over the butt of Albie's pistol, yanked it from his belt, and threw it away. Now both his hands were free for the choking.

In the angry pleasure this gave him Cernak had forgotten the sheath knife at Albie's side. He remembered it a half instant before Albie's good hand plunged the blade into his side.

Cernak grunted and cursed. A red flame ignited in his head. He put all the strength of both hands into his hold and shut his eyes. He felt the tension run out of Albie's body.

Albie's hand slipped from the knife haft. His knuckles hit the table with a nerveless thud.

Cernak opened his eyes. Growling in his

throat, he let go of Albie and reared back, staggering, grabbing at the knife between his ribs.

The handle was slick with blood, and he had to freshen his hold twice before he could wrench it free. Doubled up with pain, he pressed his hands over the gushing wound and drew himself upright. A red mist clouded his eyes.

Albie was stretched on his back across the table, legs dangling over the edge. His head was back and his mouth hung open. That was all for Albie. But maybe all for Anton Cernak too. *Eh!* Had he let a dumb lunkhead do for him?

"Grandpa, grandpa!"

Laddie was clasping him around the legs. Cernak shook away the red, floating mist and settled down on his heels and held the little boy. Funny. He had not held his grandson till now.

"Where were you?" he asked in Russian.

"In the room where Little Mother and I sleep. Grandfather —"

"Here, here," Cernak rumbled, holding him at arm's length. "No crying now. You have been brave; be brave a little longer, eh? Where is your mother?"

"I don't know." The boy fought to stifle his sobs. "Last night she went out in the storm. She did not come back."

Cernak stared at the boy for a long disbelieving moment. *Anna,* he thought. *My girl. My girl* . . .

The pained shock of it fuzzed away on the stabbing agony that filled his side. Anna. Lost in storm. Search? What good now? Think of getting small Laddie out — away from here — nothing else.

"Where are your coat and boots, boy? Get them quick."

Still holding one hand pressed tight over his side, Cernak got his Winchester from the pile of guns in the corner. Going back to the kitchen then, he dug swiftly through a drawer and came out with a box of .45-70 shells. The Winchester's magazine was full — fifteen shots and one chambered and Cernak was a hunter; the rifle was his weapon — so he could ram the fresh box of cartridges into his coat pocket for reserve.

He also opened his shirt and plastered a handful of flour over the wound, then wadded a towel above that and buttoned his shirt over it.

Laddie came from the off-kitchen cubbyhole, carrying the small capote and boots that Anna had made for him. Anton quickly bundled him up, then lifted him into the crook of his arm. Even the boy's little weight caused a fresh dagger of pain to slash at his side.

"Hold on tight, boy," Anton muttered as he opened the kitchen door. "Now we run for it."

Nobody had ever described George Shallot as robust. Even as a boy and a young man, he had been slight almost to frailty. Wasted by slow disease for the past five years, his toleration for cold weather and physical exertion had never been lower. He tired more quickly than ever these days; his coughing fits came more frequently and were worse than he had ever known.

Yet, driving himself with a fury through the long dawn hours, he came close to overtaking Anton Cernak on the trail down from the old Corona works. As long as he clung to the trail's outer rim, the lack of snowshoes presented no problem. He was taking a bitter risk and didn't care. To traverse the slick-blown rock over a dropaway would be foolhardy in any case. When a man pushed himself so furiously that he was half blind and stumbling, it was near insanity.

A core of bloody pain ate at the center of

his chest. Even his coughing had dissolved to a husky rasp because his throat muscles could no longer force a real sound. Time and again his legs gave way, plunging him on his hands and knees. Several times his feet slipped on the rimrock, nearly throwing him into the gulf. Each time he saved himself by pitching his body sideways into the banked snow on the inner trail.

Ahead of him, Cernak had set a steady but not driving pace. And finally, coming out on a spur of rock high above Thirty Mile, Shallot could look down and see the Polack, a small moving dot that had almost achieved the bottom of the pass.

It didn't seem far, but Shallot knew he was still many minutes from the bottom. Cernak had that many minutes to put whatever plan he had into motion. And Shallot had already driven himself beyond his ordinary limits. He was scraping his last residue of will. He could feel it in the anguished ache of his body, in the torpid slush of his thoughts.

He didn't even think about it. The floundering drive of his legs carried him off the spur, down the slope, in a pitching, wobbling run. He simply worked his lurching legs and let momentum carry him. Downhill all the way, that was something.

His foot snagged; he fell but did not stop. Somersaulting a dozen feet, he slammed on his side and rolled another dozen. Even then he did not pause, scrambled up to his hands and knees, lifting his bruised body to another spurting run before he fell again. This time he skidded on his side and was brought up with a teeth-jarring impact against a rocky abutment.

When he crawled to his feet again, Shallot thought he had broken a couple of ribs. He ground his palm furiously against his side, testing. No. The flesh felt scraped and pummeled was all. Later his body would pay the brutal toll of this. Now his only concern was to stop Cernak.

Nevertheless, he tackled the rest of the descent more carefully. No good battering himself senseless.

Halfway down, Shallot paused for a short rest, bracing his hips against a boulder. He focused his eyes with difficulty. Cernak, he saw, was no longer in sight below. By now he was among the buildings and turning that shrewd Polack brain to use.

Shallot kept going. After a small eternity of staggering and falling and sliding, he halted again. Not over a hundred yards to go now, but without a few minutes' rest he couldn't go another foot. He lay in the snow and studied what he could see of the old buildings, silent in the windy dawn. Goddam! What was the Polack up to?

Suddenly a single shot. It bucketed ringing echoes along the line of buildings. Shallot reared up to his feet, then fell on his hands and knees with a groan.

He waited dismally, trying vainly to make out what was going on. No use. The overgrowth of young pine mantling the lower slope cut off too much of his view. He listened helplessly to a short drumroll of exploding bullets. What was that? He had to get down there now.

With the aid of a pine trunk, he inched himself upright. He held onto the tree till his legs steadied. Then he moved on painstakingly, floundering from one tree to the next.

The trees ended, and he was behind the buildings toward the west end of Thirty Mile. The shots had come from his end — or had seemed to. Now he could hear men's excited voices. Dolph's and Cullin's, they sounded like.

Shallot fumbled out his pistol and slogged on. He passed through an alley and came out onto the street.

Dolph and Cullin were just emerging

from one of the buildings, their guns out, heads turning warily. Seeing him, they hauled up in surprise. Dolph came over at his grasshopper lope, a shotgun swinging in his fist.

"Captain, was that you shooting?"

Shallot managed a rasping whisper. "I was about to ask you the same."

"You just got back? Where's Quintus? Where's the —"

"Quintus is dead. Polack killed him and got away. He's here now . . . Polack. Must have fired — damn it, did you leave the station unguarded?"

"Nope. Albie, he there."

"Where the hell is Milt?"

"Polack gal went out in the storm last night. Milt went after her. Neither of 'em's come back. Billy . . . preacher tried to save him, but Billy, he dead."

Shallot swore. His mind was clicking furiously now, his exhaustion forgotten.

"Listen. Cernak has the money. Now he'll try to get his grandson and clear out. Those shots — must have been to pull you away —"

"Hell, man, we come on the run out here, Cull and me. If the Polack had made for the station, we should o' seen him. He got to be in one o' these places —"

"Damn it, look for his tracks! There are no tracks here! Look behind the buildings across the way —"

"Over here!" Cullin yelled.

He was standing by an old shed, beckoning. They went over. Smoke was oozing from a score of cracks in the warped boards.

"Open the door," Shallot snarled.

Dolph nudged it open with a cautious foot. A sooty billow puffed out. Dolph went in swiftly, his gun pointed. A moment later he backed out, coughing, clutching a bandanna over his nose.

He guessed, he said, that Cernak had pulled a trick with a little fire and some bullets. Looked that way to him anyhow.

"Get to the station," Shallot husked. "No — wait. Dolph to the station. Cullin, cover the livery barn. He'll try for the horses next. Go on! Don't wait for me!"

The two men headed back down the street. Shallot followed, dragging one foot after the other. His body was totally spent, but as long as his brain functioned, so would his body after a fashion.

Suddenly the hulking shape of a man came into view from the station, angling out on the street at a labored run. Cernak, his grandson slung up in his arm, was heading for the livery.

Shallot stopped and lined his pistol on the slow, bearlike form. He began shooting carefully, his bullets kicking up the powdery snow to Cernak's left and right.

The ordinary Colt's feats of accuracy were confined to Buntline's yellow-backed thrillers. At this range, Shallot knew even as he fired, the best marksman in the world couldn't hope for better than a twenty-four-inch group.

There was an odd, listing sway to Cernak's gait. He was hurt. Albie, Shallot thought. He must have got Albie but hadn't come off unscathed. The wound was slowing him. Dolph and Cullin had started running toward the Polack as soon as he'd hit the street. Cullin was pumping shots jerkily, wildly.

Dolph halted and brought up the shotgun. Cernak had nearly reached the barn, and perhaps this caused Dolph to fire too quickly.

The Greener bellowed. The shot made a raking, ineffectual splatter against the barn door, feet to Cernak's right. As he reached the door Cernak suddenly wheeled, set his grandson down, and dropped to one knee. He whipped up his Winchester and worked the lever rapid-firing.

Shallot threw himself down in the snow, flattening out. Dolph and Cullin, seeing Cernak's intent at once, had veered off to the side. Now Dolph yelled and plunged on his face. A moment later he scrambled up and hobbled on, his leg awkward.

Cullin had already dodged into an alley between a pair of dilapidated buildings, and Dolph joined him there.

Cernak seized up his grandson, pulled open the barn door, and lunged inside. Swiftly then he dragged the door shut.

Shallot crawled to his feet and ducked low as he moved painfully down the street toward the alley. He went as fast as he could for in a few more seconds Cernak could commandeer any of numerous cracks or knotholes in the front wall. With a final stumbling effort he made the alley and was shut off from any angle of fire.

Dolph was sitting in the snow with his back to the weathered boards, rolling up his pantsleg above his half boot. Blood was trickling from holes on either side of his knotty calf.

"Dirty sonofabitch!" he swore. He picked up the shotgun and glared at it and snarled, "Useless goddam piece o' junk." He flung it savagely against the side of the other building. He dug out a dirty bandanna to tie around his calf.

"We got that Polack boxed anyways," Cullin said, punching the spent loads out of his .45. "Trouble is, he don't come out, but we don't go in neither."

"He'll come out," Shallot said through his teeth. "He likes a fire so goddam well. We'll build him one."

18

Raven came to with an odd buzzing in his head, and on his spine, a weird cold trickle. He realized he was lying in the snow on his back. Partly anyway. Anna's face was bent above him. She was kneeling behind him and had pulled him partly upright, her thighs supporting his head and shoulders. She was resting his head between her hands, rolling it gently side to side, giving it a hard little slap now and then.

"Milt!" she said urgently.

Raven groaned. He braced both hands against the ground and pushed himself up to a sitting position. That chill sensation slithered down his back — nothing but snow that had got inside his collar. But the damned buzzing continued. Another thing — a sudden blurring and darkening of his sight. It passed in a moment, but everything had an odd appearance — frayed and misty and unreal.

He passed a hand over his scalp. His fingers came away red and sticky. He felt again, ignoring the raw blaze of pain, and determined that his skull was intact. But he felt dizzy and strangely remote from things, and the annoying fuzz clung to his vision.

At the moment there was nothing much to see. He had been coming around the rear end of the stacks when Cernak had shot him. He was still where he had fallen. The towering lumber piles cut off their view of the station and the street.

"Milt." Anna's hands were gripping his shoulders. "You no hurt bad?"

"Don't know," he muttered. "You see your pa?"

"What?"

"He was here. Shot me."

"But how he get away!"

"Dunno. He was crouching right over there. Those are his tracks. I came up on him quick. Fool thing, that. I was still the enemy to him. So he shot me."

"Oh —"

There was a sudden crackle of gunfire from the direction of the street. And Raven heard a man yelling. It sounded like Shallot.

He had to find out what was going on.

He tried to get his feet under him. A trembling weakness seized him. He sank back on his heels.

The rattle of pistol and rifle shots was punctuated by the blast of a shotgun. Then the gunfire ended. "Anna, what's that . . . that shooting?"

"I no see."

"But when I was out — anything happen?"

"I not know. Only this. In hotel I heard one shot. Then three shots very quick. I run out. I see your brother and black man come from station. I run quick back of building so they no see me. I come this way to reach station. I worry for Laddie. I come on you lay in snow."

Raven crouched with his head down, mustering the ginger for another try at getting up. Anna gripped his shoulders, ready to help.

How long had he been out? Not over a few minutes, he was sure. All he knew was that Cull had escaped freezing and had got back to the station. Also that Shallot and Cernak (and Terrill, he supposed) had returned. Cernak had gotten away somehow and was armed. Now somebody — or several parties — were shooting. Had been.

"Milt!" Again urgent pressure in her

hands. "We must go to station! We must get my boy. Maybe this be chance, eh? Maybe they all on street."

Raven gave a sluggish nod. "Right. Get to station. Get your boy . . . preacher and his wife too, they want to come. We got to try to get to the stable . . . horses. Give me a hand."

Anna braced her weight and held tight. Leaning heavily on her, Raven maneuvered shakily to his feet. The world pinwheeled. Nausea hit him. He swallowed hard and forced his feet to move.

They went slowly between the lumber stacks and came to the end, and now they stood in sight of the station. Cernak had been crouching here when Raven had surprised him. The line of Cernak's tracks led away across the intervening lots to the station's rear.

Cernak must have had the same idea they did, Raven thought. Had he gotten the boy out? Silence held on the street now, and from here you couldn't tell what might be happening. Anyway they should check in the station first.

His legs had steadied. "Think I can make it alone," he said. "Let go of me. But stay close."

He got his gun out and tramped slowly

toward the station. Anna walked beside him, watchful as a brood hen.

Watching him kept her attention off the tracks. She didn't notice them till she and Raven reached the station's back door. The fresh prints led across the threshold. And another set of tracks, also Cernak's, cut back out. But he'd been running as he'd left, headed for the street.

Anna stared downward, her eyes dilating. Then she yanked open the door and ran inside, calling her son's name.

Raven plunged into the kitchen after her, grabbing her arm. "Hold it. We don't know what —"

She jerked away, then hurried into the little off-kitchen bedroom. "Ladislas! Laddie!" She came out again, eyes frantic, and ran into the common room.

Raven heard her muffled shriek. He lunged into the next room, his gun up. Anna stood with her fingers pressed over her mouth, staring at the table.

Albie lay across it on his back, legs dangling. His gaze fixed sightlessly on the ceiling.

Raven crossed to the table. He saw the purplish discolorations on Albie's throat. He'd been strangled with a terrible force. His right hand, lying open on the table, was stained with blood, apparently not his own.

Raven glanced at the floor, seeing a dark freckling of blood on the planks. He stooped and picked up the bloody knife, which he recognized as Albie's own. He glanced up at Anna.

"Your pa surprised Albie, I reckon. Maybe Albie surprised him too. Stabbed him anyway. No saying how bad —"

"Laddie!" Anna screamed.

Her eyes were wild. She started running toward the front door. Raven caught her as she was fumbling up the latch. He grabbed her shoulders and whirled her to face him.

"You ain't going out there! I'll —"

"You no stop me! Let go!"

She lashed out at his face with a fist. Raven caught her wrists and twisted her around, pulling her against his chest, locking his big arms so that Anna's were pinned at her sides. He couldn't let her run out onto the street, a target for Cullin's anger.

She writhed and kicked, sobbing bitterly. The exertion of holding her roused a battering ache in his head.

And it happened again. The darkening and blurring of his eyes. A weakness seized his muscles. He was losing his hold on the twisting, struggling woman.

Anna's furious strength threw him off balance. The two of them crashed to the floor, all of her weight coming solidly on him. Raven grunted with the jarring agony in his skull, but he kept his arms wrapped around her.

He rolled sideways and then hard over, rapping Anna's forehead against the floor. Her muscles relaxed. She didn't stop fighting but was stunned, her strength diluted.

Raven dragged himself up on his knees, pinned her with a knee against her back, yanked up both her hands behind her. He tore the scarf off his hat and used it to tie her hands. Afterward he carried her to the wall bench, set her down and bound her feet together with his belt.

A little noise pulled his glance. Aimee Parnell stood in the doorway leading to the annex.

"Mr. Raven . . . we thought — what is this? Is Anna hurt? What are you doing?"

The sight of her jarred him. She still wore that brown linen dress. It was spattered with the rusty stains of the gory operation yesterday, but he had seen those.

What he saw now was that the dress had been torn almost to shreds — fastened at the shoulders with pins. Her hairdo hung down in glossy straggles; there was a small bruise on her cheekbone.

And Cullin had been back here. He knew before he asked.

Cullin.

Cernak crouched by a knothole in the barn's front wall, just to the left of the big double doors. What the devil were they doing?

He had put his eye to the knothole just in time to see Shallot duck into the alley. Then he could not see any of them. Several minutes had passed and they'd made no other move.

What he would do in Shallot's place would be to put a man in the building across the way, send him in by the back, and station him up front. The barn had no rear doors. If the quarry tried a break, he'd be cold meat for the watcher across the way.

"Grandpa," Laddie whispered.

Cernak twisted a glance over his shoulder. The boy's eyes were big and shiny in the gloom of the stall where Cernak had made him crouch down.

"Yes, boy."

"Is my Little Mother dead?"

"I don't know, boy." He spoke with unintentional roughness. "I am afraid she is."

The little boy began to cry very softly. Not sobs of fear now. Just a lost, heartbroken crying. Cernak shifted on his aching haunches, keeping a hand flattened over the steady agony in his side, and put his eye back to the hole.

How was it to be five years old and be told that a mother was dead? Death! At five it was only a word — maybe a frightful sense of losing but not an understood thing. He remembered that much of his own father's death when he was six.

Cernak tensed. His fingers tightened around the Winchester set across his thighs. He'd been right. That had been a dim, moving wink of steel between the boards of the nailed-up window across the street. A man with a gun.

One man only? If so, the other two would be up to something. He'd find out soon enough.

He was surprised that Shallot had arrived so close behind him. But Shallot was as much a driven man as he; he knew that. He would drive just as hard to get his hands on the sacked loot whose flat, solid bulge Cernak could feel against his left arm under his coat.

Maybe Shallot would make it, too. A hell of a pickle. Cernak felt a cold disgust at the way of things. If they'd held off discovering his ruse a few more minutes, he'd now be heading down the pass, driving the horses ahead of him, Laddie on the saddle in front . . . Hell. No use making excuses. The ruse had been a clumsy one. It had deserved to fail.

He had it in his mind to bargain with Shallot for the boy's life and safety. But he'd wait till he saw what they were up to.

For himself he had no hope. But an iron stubbornness wouldn't let him surrender. He would get out with his life *and* the money. Or he would die here.

What the hell were they up to?

Anton caught a rustle of noise from a rear corner of the barn. In silence he eased to his feet, grimacing at the sharpening pain. Cold wetness rubbed against his thighs; his pants and underwear were soaked with his blood.

"Grandpa —"

Cernak touched a finger to his lips, and the boy was quiet. Weight on the balls of his feet, Cernak moved deeper into the barn. He was puzzled by a new sound, a quick, sharp scratching.

But a sudden crackling then, and he

knew. Brush had been stacked against the outside corner, a match struck. Now the flames were taking quickly.

Cernak fired into the chinking between the logs. Daylight splintered through. He heard retreating bootsteps, a mocking laugh. Dolph's voice: "Polack man! You like fires, hey — here's a fine big one for you!"

Cernak dropped down by the slot he had shot in the clay chinking. He flinched back. The flames were climbing fast. He smashed savagely at the old logs with his rifle butt, but they held solid. The fire was less than a foot away — a little blaze he could have easily stamped out.

Raging, he lurched across the barn to a trove of tools, broken and discarded, that he'd piled long ago in an empty stall. He seized on a handleless shovel with the swift, mad thought of digging out under the rear wall.

The hell. It would take too long. He slung the shovel aside. His eye fell on a rusty hand ax. The haft was split and would probably break in two if he hit too hard. Anyway, same hitch. Chopping through would take too long.

Muttering to himself, he stumbled back to the front and peered out the knothole.

No sign of them. But they were hidden, waiting. They wouldn't take a chance of rushing the barn. Not when they had only to wait for the smoke and the flames to drive him out.

"Grandpa!"

"Quiet, quiet."

Cernak stalked back up the runway again and paced around the rear wall, beating a fist here and there on the logs.

The crumpled-paper rattle of flames was louder. Smoke was spewing into the barn, rolling in gray trickles through gaps in the chinking.

Cernak furiously slammed a foot against a base log. The spongy give in the wood startled him. He knelt and ran his fingers over the damp crumbly grain. Rotten as hell here. The two logs just above were as bad.

He got the rusty hatchet and squatted down by the place, attacking the three logs with a grunting fury. He could hit with all his strength and not risk being heard, for the blade made only damply muffled *thunks* in the rotten pine. The outer wood split away in great, brittle chunks. Then he reached the sounder heartwood, and the going was tougher.

Now smoke was gushing into the barn in

thick, strangling puffs, fanning out in grayish strata. The horses were shuffling nervously.

Laddie began coughing, gagging on the smoke.

"Down on your belly, boy," Cernak grunted, not breaking the rhythm of his chopping. "Put your face to the floor. Keep it there."

He had to hurry. He was dizzy from loss of blood, pumping out more with the effort of each blow. Quickly tiring too. Weaker by the moment. Had to break through soon . . .

The horses were whickering madly, surging back and forth in their stalls, striking with their hoofs at the gates.

Cernak mopped a palm over his dripping face and blinked his stinging, watering eyes, staring about. He couldn't see flames yet, but their ominous spitting was turning to a sullen roar as the fire shot to the roof. The heat beat at his body in sultry waves.

Again he smashed at the wall. Again. He would make it. If the split handle didn't break.

The blade sank through. A section of log broke away. He was past the tough core; the weak outer shell crumbled easily to his blows. He worked feverishly to enlarge the hole. Fresh air poured against his face, steadying him. The edges of the aperture cracked off in fist-sized chunks.

He flung the hatchet aside and crawled over to Laddie. The boy lay half-conscious, convulsed by harsh retchings from smoke he'd swallowed.

Cernak heaved him across a shoulder and moved back on hands and knees to the hole and thrust the boy out into the snow. He pitched his Winchester out too. Then he wormed into the breach, twisting and wiggling his massive shoulders and trunk through.

For some moments Anton lay sprawled in the cooling snow, face down. Finally, moving very slowly, he got to his feet and stooped to pick up Laddie. Now he would carry the boy back into the pines and wait. Let those fools think the two of them were buried under a pile of blazing timbers.

"Don't bother, Polack. We'll take care of the boy."

Cernak straightened painfully, turning his head. Shallot stood less than a dozen yards away, his pistol casually leveled.

A red blossom of rage burst in Cernak's brain. That goddam little consumptive had outthought him.

Shallot chuckled quietly. "Think I'd take

any more chances with you? Now get the money out. Drop it. I don't want it ruined by the bullet."

Cernak slowly unbuttoned his coat. Then he plunged his hand in and down, past the money sack stuffed inside his coat, to the .45 rammed in his belt.

Shallot, hardly moving at all, fired. A blow like a powerfully flung boulder slammed Cernak in the chest. He rocked back, stumbled forward, pitched to the ground.

With a vast, clawing effort he made it back to his knees.

Shallot shot him again.

Cernak's face dropped in the snow. It was all coolness then, pain fading, cool turning swiftly to cold. And a great, sighing darkness.

19

Raven heard the shots as he came running from the roadhouse toward the burning barn. All he could see was smoke spewing from the roof in great, oily billows. Then he saw Dolph come limping out of the building across the way, heading for the barn too. Dolph saw him and halted; his jaw fell in surprise. As Raven reached him Dolph growled, "Man, you look live enough to me."

"What the hell is it?"

Dolph nodded at the barn. "We-all trapped the Polack in there. Little kid is with him. Must be passed out from smoke, the both —"

"Come on!" Raven yelled the words. And Dolph was close behind him.

They dragged open the barn door and plunged into the strangling fog of smoke. Wind looped through the runway, half dissipating the fumes. A draft?

As the smoke began clearing, Raven saw a jagged hole chopped through the back wall. He and Dolph hurried from stall to stall, he searching for Cernak and the boy — Dolph, for the money, no doubt.

Apparently man and boy and money had gotten out. That left the horses. Raven hollered his thought at Dolph, who nodded that he'd help.

They took opposite sides of the runway, working from the back of the barn to the front. One by one they opened the gates and hurrahed the frantic animals down the runway, out the door. The fire hadn't advanced too far; they were able to get every animal out without a blindfold.

By the time they'd driven the last animal into the street, the heat was riding against them in blistering gusts. The bodies of the stockboy and Mendez remained inside, but Raven and Dolph had had all they could take. They stumbled from the barn and grabbed up handfuls of snow to press against their raw eyes.

Raven wondered where Cullin was. Shallot. Cernak and the boy. He'd find out directly.

"Whew." Dolph rubbed his eyes clean with his bandanna. "Man, I don't see how you still alive —"

"We were lucky."

"Polack gal come through too, eh?"

"Yeah. I found her all right."

"Ain't that something," said Cullin, chuckling.

Raven turned, blinking his eyes partly clear. Cullin was standing on the porch of the tumbledown store that faced the livery barn. His gun was in his fist.

Aimee Parnell had told Raven what had happened with her and her husband. He was grateful that it hadn't been worse, but it was bad enough. Cullin was completely beyond control. He had attacked two women within a space of twelve hours.

You made a mistake, all right, leaving him to freeze last night, Raven thought. *You should have shot him on the spot.*

"Yeah," Cullin said. "You and that tough Polack gal. Tell us about that, Milt."

He started to bring up the gun.

Dolph's hand dipped into his deep coat pocket and whipped up a spare pistol. "You leave it be, man. We got troubles enough."

"I made myself a promise about you too, nigger."

"You looking to keep it now, boy," Dolph said, "you gonna run out your own string too."

"Quit that," Shallot said sharply.

He tramped slowly into sight from around the barn, a Winchester rifle in one fist, an oilcloth sack in the other. He was in dismal shape; he looked half frozen. But a bright pleasure filled his eyes. Raven made a guess at the sack's contents.

"Hullo, Milt. Made it through the storm, eh? Dolph tell you? — the Polack killed Quintus. But I got the Polack and his —"

"Where's the boy?" Raven cut in.

Shallot eyed him with a hard, narrow smile. "As I was saying, I got the Polack and his stealings." He tapped the sack and then nodded backward. "Kid's back there. He's not hurt."

Raven hurried back of the barn.

He found Laddie kneeling in the snow beside Cernak, who was stretched on his face. "Grandpa, Grandpa," the boy sobbed, tugging at Cernak's coat.

Raven dropped to one knee and carefully rolled Cernak on his back, then opened his coat and drenched shirt. He found a faint, off-threading pulse, but Cernak was done for. The stab in his ribs was deep and serious, but the two holes in his chest — so close together that a hand would cover both — had settled the matter.

"Can't do nothing for your grandpa,

Laddie. You come along now."

"No!" The boy was sobbing unrestrainedly, but his voice stayed clear and firm. "I stay with Grandpa."

"Your mama's back there. Want to see her, don't you? She wants to see you."

Laddie raised his fierce, tearful eyes, meeting Raven's for a doubtful moment. "Mama?"

"Sure."

The boy held out his arms, and Raven picked him up and carried him back to the street. The three men looked at him.

"Daddy Milt," Cullin jeered.

"Watch it," Dolph said flatly, and nodded toward the roadhouse.

Anna was coming out, a rifle in her hands. One of theirs. She had managed to free herself, or Aimee had freed her — though Raven had asked her not to.

Raven shuttled a hard glance at the others. "I'll handle this. Any of you wants it otherwise, he can try me first."

Shallot nodded. "All right, Milton. Your game. But get that rifle away from her or the game will get rough."

Anna had come to a stop in the middle of the street, both hands clenched around the rifle. Her tall body was straight and stiff, feet apart; the wind whipped her skirt and hair. Anna Kosciusko made a vital, magnificent picture in her anger.

Raven walked quickly, keeping between her and the men. Anna moved forward a few steps, slowly. Then she dropped the rifle and ran to meet them, taking Laddie from him and crushing him tightly to her.

"Sorry," Raven said.

Anna looked at him across Laddie's shoulder, nodding. "I know," she whispered. "I know. Is all right. Just so my boy safe."

"Your pa is out back of the barn. They fired it and he got out, but Shallot shot him. Afraid he's done."

Her eyes darkly dilated. She went quickly on toward the barn, hugging her son to her, not even glancing at the three outlaws as she passed them. She vanished behind the barn.

Raven tramped back to the others. Shallot looked deathly tired all at once; his skin was faintly bluish with cold. His words came thick and labored.

"Dolph was just telling me. Seems some bad blood has begun in my absence. We'll be going our own ways soon enough — once the split's made. Be nice if you-all try to avoid killing each other till then. In fact,

I'll shoot any sonofabitch who starts trouble."

He gave Cullin a flat look. "Think I'll keep an eye on you. Come up to the house with me. Milt, Dolph, round up the horses. Milt, would you know what's happened to Albie?"

Raven told about Albie.

Shallot scrubbed a hand tiredly over his face. "All right. Going to rest awhile. Bring the animals up by the house. We'll be out of here inside the hour."

Anna trudged slowly into sight, holding her son very tightly. She halted and looked at Raven, her eyes dull and frozen. "He is dead."

There was nothing else to say, and she went on to the roadhouse. So did Shallot and Cullin.

Dolph said he thought that the horses hadn't drifted far in this weather; likely they had hunted shelter. He pointed. "Seen a few head back that way."

They started up an alley. Raven saw the shotgun in the snow. He halted, picked it up, and batted the snow away with his palm. Dolph clucked his tongue in disgust.

"Man, that thing no good. Clean missed on me inside a good range."

"I'll take it along anyway," Raven said.

"Always wanted a good-looking shotgun."

Dolph shrugged. "You might's well have these." He dug two boxes of shells from his pocket and handed them over.

Raven broke the gun, inspected the loads, replaced the used shell with a fresh "Double-O Buck." The two men continued up the alley.

They found the horses in a scattered group on the lee side of several buildings. After singling out their own mounts, Shallot's and Cullin's too, they led them back by the halter ropes to the roadhouse and tied them at the hitch rail.

They went inside. The fires had been built up; the heat hit their faces like damp, hot pillows. Albie's body had been dragged from the table and lay in a corner, a blanket flung carelessly over it.

Another dead man. *Five,* Raven thought. *Five! Christ!*

He had never seen so many things go wrong in such a short time. And it wasn't ended.

Parnell was standing by the table. He looked different, somehow, and Raven wasn't sure why. He was still pallid, showing the effect of nervous strain, unaccustomed drinking, and the nasty clout Cullin had fetched him.

Shallot was slumped in an armchair by the east fireplace. He made a tired gesture at the minister and smiled. "Our lamb of God has suddenly become a Christian soldier."

Cullin came from the annex, their bedrolls tucked beneath his arms. Parnell's stare found him and followed him to the door. Cullin dumped the bedrolls on the floor beside their saddles and other gear, and turned around.

"Preacher, you keep cross-eying me, I'll give you some more pretty color on the other side o' your head."

"You damned filthy coward," Parnell said quietly.

"James!" Aimee was sitting in a chair close to him, and now she rose and touched his arm. "They are going now. There's no need."

"Do you know" — Parnell bit his words off evenly as he watched Cullin — "I left Boston bearing some quite funny ideas. About Western men. The innate good under the rough. I didn't realize that a slime of pure evil can flourish anywhere. Exist of and for its own sake. Slime."

"You better get off that," Cullin said.

"Human slime," Parnell in a flat and bloodless voice. "The kind that holds a little boy to be burned. Strikes an unarmed man. Attacks helpless women. The rest of you are no whit better."

The difference in Parnell was very clear now. He had stopped being afraid. It was that simple.

Shallot's smile faded on his lips. He studied the minister with narrowing eyes but said nothing. He was looking at a man armored against anything he might say or do, and he knew it. Parnell, totally unafraid now, would be the winner. If you shot him dead, he would die having won.

The silence stretched out. Raven thought, *Preacher, don't push it, for God's sake!* You could carry this raw courage business too far.

Parnell stared at them all with a contemptuous unconcern. He didn't speak again. Didn't have to. His contempt was total, and he let them feel it.

"Doc," Dolph said, "I be proud to have you look at this here leg. Got a bootful o' blood."

Parnell said curtly, "Sit down." Dolph sat and pulled off his boot.

Raven went into the kitchen to collect some grub. Anna was kneeling on the floor beside Laddie, scrubbing at the soot and dirt on his face. Except for a hacking cough now and then, the little boy seemed no worse for his experience.

Anna raised her eyes, eyes that were dismal and grieved. "Milt," she whispered, "what you do now? You go with them?"

"No," Raven said. "Not ever again. Said so, didn't I? Anna, I got to stop Cullin riding out. He ain't fit to go free. My fault in a way he's here. He can't be let to hurt anyone else."

"But what you do?"

"Watch my chance. Want you to keep the boy in here with you. Understand?"

He scooped canned goods, bacon, flour, and coffee off the shelves and dropped them into a flour sack as he softly talked. He looked at Anna and got her sober nod. He returned to the common room.

While Shallot rested and Parnell tended Dolph's leg, the brothers carried out the saddles and cinched them on, then bridled the animals and fastened on bedrolls, saddlebags, and other gear. As they worked they didn't once look at each other or speak.

Should he wait till they were all mounted and riding out to make his move? Raven had already decided no. Getting the drop on three unsuspecting men might be no trick. Handling them afterward would be the problem. If they were on horseback, handling them would be that much harder.

It had to be now.

20

He and Cullin went back in the house. Raven said, "All ready." Shallot gripped the arms of his chair and lifted himself carefully. His legs were far from steady, and he didn't look a jot better. "On our way. Come on, Dolph."

The Negro, sitting in a chair, was doubled over rubbing his flexed leg, which Parnell had cleaned and bandaged. Raven noticed that Dolph's coat was open, which meant that he could get at his hip gun easily. And he was quick. Deadly quick. The one to watch.

Anna came to the kitchen doorway. She met Raven's eyes. He had moved casually over by the west fireplace. His vantage of the room was perfect. The shotgun was nestled in the crook of his arm, pointed floorward.

Raven moved only his eyes to warn her. His look said *Get back!* But Anna did not move at once. She pointed at the pan of dirty water Parnell had used to clean Dolph's wound.

"Aimee, you come help me in kitchen, please? Bring that."

Aimee nodded and picked up the pan. Shallot gave both women a fleeting, indifferent glance as they went into the kitchen. He was walking slowly back and forth, testing his legs. Now he moved to the door.

Here it was, Raven thought.

Anna had neatly drawn Aimee out of the room. That left the preacher, and he'd have to take his chances.

Not an ideal situation, but it would have to do. Dolph was positioned too far from the others, but Cullin, standing a few feet from the door, was close to Shallot, who was just raising the latch. *Now.*

Raven slung the shotgun up across his raised left arm and braced it. He eared back the hammers. The sounds were crisp and specific.

Shallot's eyes were pale and hooded. "Are we playing jokes, Milton?"

"Cullin's staying. So's the money. That's no joke."

Raven held the shotgun pointed halfway between Shallot and Dolph. He could swing at an instant's choice, either way.

"I think I understand." Shallot nodded slowly. "Then, we're free to ride out, Dolph and me — eh? I'd have expected better of you, Milton."

"I figure worse. Dig it out."

"I say — what a sweet caucus you and that Polack girl must have had, eh?" Shallot grinned bonily. "You're very foolish, Milton. Still . . ."

He shrugged and moved his hand toward his mackinaw pocket which bulged with the oilcloth sack. It was a moment for caution, and Raven watched the hand.

Not all of his attention was on the hand. But Dolph, gambling that it was, straightened his powerful grasshopper legs in a sudden lunge out of his chair. A sinewy hand slashed in and out of his coat.

All Raven's reflexes were keyed for the moment. The shotgun came around in a tight short arc. He pulled the right-hand trigger as Dolph's gun blurred out and up. The solid bucking blast slammed Dolph back in his chair, and his weight heaved it over. The .45 flipped in the air, free of his hand, as he went backward.

Raven had a glimpse of Parnell diving to the floor. Then he was swinging back on the door, triggering the second barrel.

Too quick. The shot exploded into the

logs on Shallot's right. And then Shallot, the latch already raised, went out the door and was gone.

It was a wrong choice for Raven. He'd known it even as he had shot. Shallot could get out the door much faster than he could bring out his gun. Cullin was the danger. He knew that too. And yet chose wrongly.

Now he held an empty shotgun. Not even a second left to drop it and reach his side gun. For Cullin's .45 was out and free and moving up, freezing on his chest. Cullin's eyes were laughing and lethal. Of this moment, he'd always remember that.

From the floor Parnell shot Cullin. The bullet hammered into him like an angry fist. He was flung with a terrible impact against the wall. He dropped off it, the gun sinking in his fist, his body slipping toward the floor.

Parnell was stretched out on his belly, and Dolph's gun was in his hand. Quite deliberately, he got to his knees, cocked the gun again, and lifted it.

Raven saw his expression. It was worthy of old Jehovah. "No," Raven whispered. It wouldn't have mattered if he'd yelled it.

Parnell brought the gun level. He fired again.

Cullin's body slammed a second time against the logs. This time he fell away in a quick buckling movement, like a puppet with all its strings cut.

Raven stumbled to him and dropped down and pulled Cullin up against his chest and rocked him gently. It was unthinking. He remembered the small boy Cull had been and how he had comforted him this way. His grief was for that boy.

Dolph lay flat on his back, his hands clamped like black spiders over his belly. Blood poured out between his fingers.

Parnell knelt beside him. "Can you move?"

"Man," Dolph sighed, "I go raising up, my guts go splash, I tell you. Get me a bottle whiskey."

There was a sound of a horse going away down the pass. Shallot had made it, Raven thought dully. Maybe all the way out. Maybe.

The last flurries of snow had died away. The wind was low. But the temperature was dropping fast. Shallot didn't worry too much about that, not yet.

He had a good horse under him and the sack of money and a one-way split on it, and for a time these things buoyed him with a wild exultance. The exhaustion ran out of him, and he kicked his mount hard down the snow-thin center of the pass toward Silverton.

The trouble was, his real resources were scraped fine. He'd been driving his weak, ravaged body on sheer nervous energy for many hours. He had gone about five miles when the familiar coughing fits seized him, doubling him with knifelike pains. He hacked up gobbets of bloody phlegm. The fever began boiling in his guts and brain.

The cold fixed cruel talons in his fingers, toes, ears. He was only a sixth of the distance to Silverton. He drummed his animal's flanks and pushed him hard, harder. The horse's efforts were labored in the snow, and Shallot could feel it. But death by freezing was worse, to him, than his mount foundering.

The horse's front hoofs skated crazily on icy rock. He crashed down on his knees. Shallot pulled him up with a savage rein and kicked him forward. The animal limped on the right front.

Shallot cursed and dismounted. He ran a hand above and around the shank. At least a pulled muscle. Well, goddammit, he would walk. And with any luck, he'd make Silverton by nightfall. If the cold grew too intense, he had matches, there was plenty of scrub pine.

He stripped off his bedroll and saddle-bags and rifle, and began tramping. For a while the exercise prickled warmth back to his extremities. Then it began to increase his exhaustion. His feet became unfeeling chunks that he woodenly lifted and set down and lifted. The cold settled achingly to his marrow. Time and again he halted to cough, the flecks of his sputum dark on the snow.

The rifle was discarded first. Another straggling hundred yards and the saddle-bags followed. They contained only minor accessories and some food for which he had no hunger. The fever burned like a hot coal in his brain. Later (he was not sure when) he became sluggishly aware that he could no longer feel his hands or his legs to the knees.

In sudden panic he beat his mittened hands against his cheeks. His face was numb. He stamped his feet, beat his hands, slapped his cheeks, felt (with a vast relief) the tingling needles of pain.

He had to rest before he dropped in his tracks. He used his last strength to climb the gorge flank for a dozen yards, to a cramped grove of white-cowled young spruce. The small trees grew in a meshed tangle, many of them dead or dying, rimming a little glade. Shallot squatted down and spread out his bedroll and sat on it, his legs drawn up and his head between his knees.

His rest had helped, but now that he'd stopped, the cold got to him quickly. He needed sleep, but to sleep safely he'd need a fire as well as his blankets.

Last night he'd started a fire with dry twigs; they'd do again. He broke off handfuls from the base trunks and arranged them, and pulled off his mitten with his teeth in order to strike a match.

The twigs took but died almost at once to fine red wires, which died too. Air was coasting in softly close to the ground, he realized — enough to wipe out a tiny flame. He clamped down a little crawling fright.

Paper. That would start it. He quickly searched his clothing. Any paper articles he possessed had been discarded with the saddlebags.

Except.

No, goddammit! Money to burn, all right. But not that way! A piece of cloth would do as well; he could hack off a patch of clothing with his jackknife. Feverishly he hunted through his pockets again.

The knife was gone. He must have lost it in one of his many falls, coming down from the mine. He tried to rip off a bit of his shirt with his teeth, but his fingers were too stiff with cold to hold the fabric for tearing.

Paper! He ripped at the oilcloth wrapping and pulled out one of the small packets. Bills in hundreds. He extracted one, wadded it under the twigs and tried to strike another match. Unable to hold it tightly enough in his fingers, he clamped it in his teeth and awkwardly struck it on the box lid.

Its flaring flung sulphurous sparks in his face, startled him into jamming it into the partly open box held between his wrists. Half a hundred sulphur-headed matches erupted into flame.

Shallot poked the blazing box into the twigs and watched the broad spoon of flame grow swiftly. The bright warmth stirred confidence; he would make it all right.

The spruce limb by his head drooped with a white burden. Now, softened by heat, a moist slab of snow slid gently off and plopped onto the fire, wiping it out.

Shallot stared aghast. He scrabbled

wildly through the wet char and saw it was hopeless. Staggering to his feet, he floundered out of the trees and started down the pass at a shuffling run.

But not toward Silverton. Back toward Thirty Mile. It was his only chance.

He felt the gun at his side. He laughed. They'd never expect his return, Raven and the others. No trick to catch them off guard. Force them to his will.

Very soon his steps slowed. His whole body was wracked with pain and fever and freezing cold. He was drunkenly weaving with exhaustion. *Tired. So damned tired.*

No. He knew what that meant. Had to fight it.

He plodded on dimly. He fell several times and barely made it to his feet. Finally he could only crawl to his hands and knees. He groaned and slipped down. With a great effort he managed to roll onto his back.

Shallot couldn't move farther. But he found with a drowsy surprise that the pain was gone. The fever hummed pleasantly in his ears. God, it was good to just lie this way with warmth stealing through him. Was this how you froze? Felt damned natural.

He thought of his tropic island. Smiled.

His hand fumbled out the oilcloth sack and crumpled it against his chest. Faraway island. Very close now. Golden heat rippled in his veins.

His hand relaxed. Gusting up, the wind fanned light snow over him, silvering the creases of his clothes. It tugged the sack sideways in his open hand. Some bills blew out. They fluttered down the pass for several yards and knifed into the banked snow and were silvered over too.

21

Raven brought Dolph the cup of whiskey he'd asked for but hesitated to let him have it. "You take this stuff with your guts all tore up, be like drinking fire."

"I don't give a shit, man. Give it here."

Raven raised Dolph's head and tilted the cup to his mouth. He drank a little, only to grimace and squeeze his eyes tightly shut.

" 'Nough, man. You was right." He sagged back in the bunk, a laugh gurgling in his throat. "Never got any too warm my whole life. Man, I warm now. I turning red-hot. That there was a pretty fair shotgun after all, seems like."

"Sorry. I'm sorry."

Dolph turned his wearily glazed eyes upward. "Man, why you sorry?"

Raven stirred his shoulders. "Had the feeling we'd started to be friends."

"Don't you worry none about that, man.

Ain't no black man and white man can be friends."

Raven straightened up, glancing toward Parnell, who was sitting by Irish O'Herlihy. The driver was sleeping again, but he had roused an hour ago and had spoken a few rational words.

The minister rose, came over to Dolph, and felt his pulse. Then shook his head. "Not long for him, I'm afraid."

"The driver?"

"Should be on his feet in a few days. May have dizzy spells for a long while, but that's the worst I'd expect. Thought for a time I'd have to operate." Parnell's mouth tightened with the shadow of a smile. "Funny thing, I believe I could. Would you step into the main room with me? I have something to say."

The two went out to the common room. The early dusk was relieved by the cheery glow of two fires. The hushed voices of the women reached from the kitchen.

Raven filled a cup from the all-but-empty keg and drank deeply, resting his elbows on the bar and glancing around the room. Amazing how quickly women's tidy hands could put things in order, glossing away the signs of passion and violence that, in forty-eight hours, had changed every life they'd touched.

He didn't want to think about most of it. Not yet. Just now it all dissolved into an unreal jumble. A man needed time, time to count all his casualties. Or disguised blessings. What the hell. He drank again.

Parnell drained the keg into a cup and took a healthy slug. He smacked his lips with unconscious pleasure and stared thoughtfully at the wall.

"How are your eyes? Any more blurring?"

"No."

"Good." Parnell rubbed the back of his neck. "I wish I could say that I'm sorry. But I'm not. I'd do it again, exactly that way, if I could."

Raven said nothing.

"What troubles me," Parnell murmured, "is how easily I did it. That gun felt as natural to my hand as a scalpel. My God, I'm a healer, not a killer. Why the devil don't you say something? The man was your brother."

"I'm listening."

"I don't know . . . unless it's that I could never care enough before. Never found a cause I'd willingly die for. Or kill for. Not literally, necessarily. Just to feel that strongly about anything. Enough to try, try again. Then I found — after what your brother did — that I had more than cause enough. Aimee. I could die for her. Kill for her. Live in hell for her and be glad of the chance. Because she's more to me than any creed, my church, my hope of heaven." He flushed a little and shook his head slowly. "That, my friend, is a hell of a thing for a minister to say."

"Not if it's the truth."

"What is the truth? The only thing I'm sure of is, I had no business — even if not for the other thing — entering the ministry. I'm not even a very damned good Christian. I always did like a stiff drink, but I gave it up. Now look at me. Hell, I'm not a drunk, but I like a drink. I killed a man. Worse. Executed him. Deserving or not, who was I to judge? Finally, I love a woman more than my sacred calling. What do you think of that?"

"Think I'd like to see you operate again. Drink to it?"

An hour later Dolph's fading pulse flickered out. His going was peaceful. Raven was glad of that much. He hadn't known much about Dolph Smith's past, but it was certain life hadn't given him a damned thing.

They sat down to a late and sketchy supper. Nobody had any appetite and nobody felt like talking.

Future plans? Nobody was saying much — yet. The Parnells thought they might tackle the thirty miles down to Silverton by horseback tomorrow if the weather wasn't too severe.

Both Parnells retired immediately after the meal, and Anna put Laddie to bed. Afterward she and Raven sat on the bench in the common room, watching the fires crumble to lurid glimmers, saying little.

He broke a long silence. "There's no flyers out for me. None I know of. I can go a free man. Maybe I should feel wrong about that, but I don't."

"No." Anna tightened her strong hand over his. "Is not wrong. Milt, you pay enough! That brother of yours. Oh — I should not —"

"It's like I told Parnell. What could I of done that was better?" His tone was bitter. "Packed my brother off to a crazy house somewhere? Best this way."

"We help you forget. Laddie and me." She was very serious. "You forget soon." She kissed him. Not a kiss of passion. Of tenderness threaded with hope. That much was more than he'd ever had.

"Got some forgetting to do yourself."

"Yes, some. Not all. Not all was bad. He tell me — my father — that all was for us, all he did. The boy and me. You think so?"

Raven figured it was about half true. But he realized why this was important to her. "Yeah. I'd say it was."

"So . . ." Anna smiled and nodded her head. "That be how Laddie remember his grandpa."

About the Author

T. V. Olsen was born in Rhinelander, Wisconsin, where he lives to this day. "My childhood was unremarkable except for an inordinate preoccupation with Zane Grey and Edgar Rice Burroughs." He had originally planned to be a comic strip artist but the stories he came up with proved far more interesting and compelling than any desire to illustrate them. Having read such accomplished Western authors as Les Savage, Jr., Luke Short and Elmore Leonard, he began to write his first Western novel while a junior in high school. He found no publisher for it until he rewrote it after graduating with a Bachelor's degree from the University of Wisconsin in 1955. The work was accepted by Ace Books and was published in 1956 as *Haven of the Haunted.*

Olsen went on to become one of the most widely respected and widely read authors of Western fiction in the second half of the twentieth century. Such early works as *High Lawless* and *Gunswift* are brilliantly plotted with a simple, powerfully evocative style and fascinating and credible characters and situations. Olsen went on to write such important works as *The Stalking Moon* and *Arrow in the Sun* which were made into classic Western films, the former starring Gregory Peck and the latter, under the title *Soldier Blue*, starring Candice Bergen. Olsen's novels have been translated into numerous European languages, including French, Spanish, Italian, Swedish, Serbo-Croat and Czech.

Any Olsen novel is guaranteed to combine drama and memorable characters with an authentic background of historical fact and an accurate portrayal of Western terrain. As has been stated in the second edition of *Twentieth Century Western Writers*, ". . . with the right press Olsen could command the position currently enjoyed by the late Louis L'Amour as America's most popular and foremost author of traditional Western novels."

We hope you have enjoyed this Large Print book. Other Thorndike, Wheeler or Chivers Press Large Print books are available at your library or directly from the publishers.

For more information about current and upcoming titles, please call or write, without obligation, to:

Publisher
Thorndike Press
295 Kennedy Memorial Drive
Waterville, ME   04901
Tel. (800) 223-1244

Or visit our Web site at:
www.gale.com/thorndike
www.gale.com/wheeler

OR

Chivers Large Print
published by BBC Audiobooks Ltd
St James House, The Square
Lower Bristol Road
Bath BA2 3SB
England
Tel. +44(0) 800 136919
email: bbcaudiobooks@bbc.co.uk
www.bbcaudiobooks.co.uk

All our Large Print titles are designed for easy reading, and all our books are made to last.